THE GREATEST
WHITE TRASH
LOVE STORY
EVER TOLD

ALSO INCLUDES
A WAR STORY
AND
THE KEY TO THE CITY

RHETT ELLIS

Literature

ISBN 0-9670631-6-7

Contact: www.shepherdsheart.info
Rhett@shepherdsheart.info

CONTENTS

THE GREATEST WHITE TRASH LOVE STORY EVER TOLD

ONE

Terra Peoples was a white trash girl. She could cuss by the time she was two, flirt by the time she was three, and drink beer by the time she was four. When she grew up, she became an exotic entertainer, as you could have guessed. We'll come to that later. Terra had sugar blonde hair, ocean blue eyes, and a smile that never worked just right. She should have had a perfect smile because unlike most of the neighborhood she had all her teeth, but her smile always seemed defective. Profound inner complexity might have been her problem, or maybe it was just plain old white trash craziness.

Terra met Benny Carpenter in kindergarten, and she hated him the first time she saw him. If you had asked her why, she could not have told you. There was nothing unusual about his appearance. He was a normal enough looking boy with short brown hair and hazel eyes, but she hated him. She hated him for twenty eight years thereafter, and she could not have explained that either.

The first time Benny Carpenter saw Terra Peoples, he loved her. It happened on the playground. Terra was holding another little girl face down in the sandbox and pulling her hair. Benny took one look at Terra and felt all the love a five year old boy could feel. He loved her then, and he loved her forever after. Profound inner complexity might have been his problem, or maybe it was just plain old white trash craziness.

TWO

I was the little girl with her face down in the sandbox. I met my two best friends for life on the first day of kindergarten. Not many people can say that, huh?

I met my first best friend when she asked me my name.

"My name is Angel Bonsecour," I told her. "What's your name?"

"Terra Peoples," she said, and then for no apparent reason she pushed me down in the sandbox, jumped on my back, and started hitting me.

A few seconds later, I felt her weight rise off me, and I rolled over. Benny Carpenter, the boy who sat behind me that morning because, the teacher said, his last name started with C and mine started with B, was pulling Terra Peoples by the arm.

"Leave me alone, you !#@$# little boy," Terra screamed, and she twisted around and started pulling his hair.

The boy wasn't trying to hurt her, that was obvious, but seeing a fellow girl in such a predicament made me feel protective, and I jumped up and pulled Terra out of his grasp and stood between the two of them. The boy just stood there smiling. Terra clawed at his face, but I kept her from him.

Suddenly, as if the idea came to each of us at the same time, we began to play with the yellow toy sand buckets and red shovels. Terra and I started making a sand castle, but Benny mostly just sat and stared at Terra.

"I was'n tryin' to hurt ya," he said after a long time.

"Shut up," Terra said. "I didn't hear nobody talkin' to

you. Go leave us alone, you !#A$ little boy."

"Okay," he said and trudged off to play with a group of boys at the sliding board. Each time he slid down, he waved at us and Terra sneered at him.

"My daddy is a truck driver," I said at one point.

"My daddy is the man on TV that tells the news," she said.

Even a five-year-old knows the sound of a bald-faced lie, but I didn't argue with her. Somehow I knew it would have hurt her to do so, and even then that was something I could not bring myself to do. I could not have put into words why I could not, but I realize now that it was because of a kind of vulnerability that she possessed. Her vulnerability was protected by a thousand layers of hard shell. One and only one thing would ever penetrate it.

THREE

We grew up in an unincorporated area of Mobile (pronounced moe-beal, emphasis on beal) County, Alabama. We got our mail from Eight Mile, but we went to school at Semmes, which means nothing to you unless you've been there, so I will tell you about the area as it was just before we started first grade.

Flash back to late summer, 1976. It's a Saturday afternoon, and the shadows are growing long. You and I are in a car. We'll say it's a Buick. No, let's shoot the moon and say it's a Caddy— a huge, canary yellow, 1976 Cadillac Eldorado convertible. We are cruising up Lott Road, and on both sides we see cheaply built houses and oddly angled trailers among the older homes that stand on what used to be small farms.

Occasionally we see empty lots with thick underbrush and tall pines, but we know those lots won't stay empty. The area is attracting new residents. Segregation is legally dead, but it is alive and well in practice, and whites are fleeing the inner city and the neighborhoods that sprang into existence during the second quarter of the twentieth century for life outside of town.

We round a curve, and to our left we see a pack of boys on bicycles. They wear cut-off blue jeans and nothing else—no shirts, no shoes, and probably no underwear. Their hair is damp, and mud is on their legs, and we guess they've been swimming in a creek or pond down one of the dirt roads.

Suddenly a stone flies out of the pack, whizzes toward the Caddy and hits the windshield, leaving a round dimple with spider legs that, we're sure, will grow longer until the windshield will have to be replaced. We stop the car and back into a driveway, but before we can turn around we notice that the pack has vanished into the woods and we decide that searching for the guilty party would be a waste of time.

We pull back onto the road and continue our journey. A couple of miles later we see two scrawny men, each standing on opposite sides of the road. They are wearing white, grease-stained tee-shirts, jeans, and work boots. They are screaming at each other. This is too interesting to miss so we stop a few yards beyond them and listen.

Their words are loud and filthy. Each man is daring the other to cross the road and start it, if he thinks he's man enough, but neither does. We ask some kids who have congregated near a mailbox what it's about, and they say one of the men said something mean about the other one's wife on the C.B. radio, but we know it's really not about that.

These are early post-industrial age men, the soon-to-be-orphaned sons of machines. At the factories by the river, they've been selling their sweat for a week, and they just need to scream at somebody, anybody. That's all.

One of the men turns and yells, "Hey, what're ya'll lookin' at? Ya'll think you're better than us in your big fancy car?"

We know it's time to move along now so off we go. As we drive, you comment on the smell of beer and barbeque that comes to us on the breeze from time to time. Folks are cooking out, and it makes our mouths water. We decide to stop at the barbeque trailer parked beside Greer's food store at the intersection of Lott and McRary.

You order chicken, and I order pork ribs. We sit at one of the wooden picnic tables. At the far end of our table, three men are chomping potato chips, sipping tea, and talking about Alabama football. The state of Alabama is last in education, economic development, and average family income but first in football. Football is all they talk about, and the talk always drifts to one subject: The Bear.

At another table, two grown women, two teenage girls, and one small girl are eating barbeque and licking their fingers. They are wearing jeans cut short and frayed so as to draw attention to what they cover and thin tee-shirts that reveal more than they hide. All of them, even the little girl, smell of beer, cigarettes and hairspray. They notice our car and tell us how much they like it. The little girl is Terra Peoples.

When we finish our meal, we continue our drive. We pass a Baptist church, and a revival meeting is in progress. We pull into the parking lot, approach one of the open windows, and listen. It's the last night of the meeting and emotion is running high. Sinners are weeping at the altar, and the preacher is calling for others to repent.

The preacher, Brother Edwards, is not a polished seminary graduate. He works at a pulp mill on weekdays and preaches on nights and weekends. We'd better get ready, he tells us. Jesus is coming back to this fallen world to make things right, and we'd better be ready ahead of time. We'd better get saved. The preacher is a bit fanatical and half of what he says is rooted in the popular theology proclaimed by the hellfire and damnation radio preachers he adores—nothing deep or thought provoking, just straight up "get right or get burned." The preacher isn't a bad fellow, though, and more than one drowning soul has been rescued by his simple but potent brand of religion.

There's little Benny Carpenter on the front row. His daddy is dead, and his mama is at work. With the other boys and girls from his trailer park, Benny rode the church bus that the preacher's wife drives.

A mile later, we turn down a freshly paved road where new houses are going up. With vinyl and brick facades, they are larger and nicer than most of the houses we've passed. This is where the upwardly mobile families in the area are moving, trying desperately, but not successfully, to convince themselves they are not white trash, and my family is one of them. And there I am, the younger version of me, all clean and pretty in a new outfit, playing with the girl next door, the daughter of a teacher. The girl's family has just moved into the neighborhood, and she's got lots of toys. She's smart and she knows lots of games.

She's teaching my small self how to do a handclap with a song. I'm having fun, but if I had my way, I would be playing with my friend from kindergarten, Terra Peoples. She's more fun. Mama has assured me that I will see Terra again when school starts back in a few weeks, and I can hardly wait.

The teacher's daughter and my small self notice the big yellow car, and we talk about how pretty it is. She goes inside her house to get a yellow car from her doll collection.

My small self notices the crack on the Cadillac's windshield, and I imagine how it could have gotten there—maybe a pellet gun, maybe somebody threw a rock. If it was a rock, which boy threw it? I could have named several suspects, some of them as young as I. The one boy I could not have named, however, was Benny. Benny was never the type to throw stones.

FOUR

I loved them because they were a mystery to me. Even at six, I understood life's timid middle path, and as I had been reared to do, I walked it. Terra and Benny walked other paths.

During our first week of first grade, the voice of the principal came over the intercom announcing a fire drill. The teacher told us what to do, and without thinking about it, I got in line to march outside. Terra, who had witnessed a fire in her trailer park and for whom fire held almost mythic associations, began to panic.

"What is a fire drill?" she asked in a trembling voice.

"When a fire strikes a school," the teacher explained as we walked to the playground, "the students have to leave the building. That's why we call this a fire drill."

The teacher neglected to mention that there was no fire, and her explanation only served to terrify Terra. She began to cry and run her hands up and down her face and through her hair. The teacher ignored her. Terra and I were standing beside each other, and I asked what was wrong.

"My mama got me some crayons and some paper and some scissors, and they're in a box in my desk, and they're gonna get burned."

I felt bad for her, but I understood the situation no better than she, and I could offer no words of comfort.

"Why's she crying?" Benny asked me.

"Cause her colors and papers are going to get burned," I told him.

"Where are her colors and papers?"

"In the box in her desk."

Without saying a word, Benny darted out of the playground area and back into the building. He moved so fast that our teacher, who was talking to another teacher, didn't notice.

I had a vague sense that a fire drill was not the same thing as an actual fire since the children in the higher grades were laughing and enjoying the experience, but I knew that even if the fire had been real, even if it had been a raging blaze with flames shooting a hundred feet into the sky, Benny still would have run into that building to retrieve her crayons and papers.

He returned to the playground a few seconds later, holding all of Terra's things in his hands.

Terra saw him, approached him, and started yanking, slapping, and snatching her belongings away from him.

"Give me my stuff, you stupid $#!#@ boy. Don't you ever touch my %^&! stuff, you $*^% boy! I'll kill you if you touch my stuff!"

Her papers scattered in the breeze. Some were blown against the playground fence. I helped her pick them up. Benny smiled, and I could tell he wanted to help, but

14

having been forbidden to do so, he just stood there.

When recess came that day, I played more with Benny than I did with Terra. She pretended to ignore us and played by herself.

She could have played with the other kids, but she had beaten up each of them at least once during kindergarten, and none of them wanted to be her friend. She sulked until at last Benny went off to play with a group of boys, and I returned to playing with her.

FIVE

Terra's standing as an outsider changed. She made herself popular with our class through the same attribute of character that made her an outsider at first—her cruelty. To her cruelty she added subtlety and strategy, and by so doing she established herself as the most powerful girl in third grade. Her tactic was simple. Like a lioness studying her prey, she studied the weaknesses of our classmates, and she led in the persecution of those weaknesses. A medieval inquisitor could not have doled out more mental torture.

One girl in our class seemed to have it all working against her. It was as if the universe had conspired to make the girl miserable. Terra zealously joined the conspiracy. The girl was a slow reader so Terra called her a dumb $@#. The girl was no good at games on the playground so Terra called her a clumsy $@#. The girl was fat so Terra called her a fat $@#. The girl was always whining and crying so Terra called her a sad $@#.

When Terra started the teasing, the other children

joined her. For them it was a way of denying their own weaknesses, and if Terra affirmed a particular child's mocking skills by laughing along, that child felt very good about himself.

In this way, Terra divided and conquered. To be Terra's comrade was to be popular, was to sit in the upper seats of the elementary school society.

Benny's social standing was a good one, but it was the opposite of Terra's. Terra never found anything specific in Benny's makeup to persecute. He was a good student. He was fairly athletic, and although he was not the cutest boy, he was not bad looking. He never made one of those unfortunate mistakes, like wetting his pants or falling head first into the mud puddle at the bottom of the sliding board, that can earn a student years of scorn and possibly ruin an entire life as the first bad link in a long chain of misfortune.

Terra called him names and tried to hurt him any way she could, but her efforts never achieved their intended effect. When she ridiculed some children, the others would join her. When she ridiculed Benny, he just shook his head and laughed, and no one joined her.

"Don't you laugh at me," she would say. "I'll kill you for laughing at me. I ain't stupid."

"I don't think you're stupid," he would say. "I'm just laughing 'cause you're fun."

Benny had his own circle of friends. Some of them were those Terra ridiculed hardest, but there were others. By fifth grade, most of the boys organized and played games of football or baseball, and the girls separated into twos or threes and walked about, gossiping.

Benny and his group, however, preferred the swing sets. There was no competition there, but if there had been, Benny would have won it. They swung so fast and so high that the swings often went higher than the swing sets' top bar, causing the swings to whip and twist out of control. Sometimes when they swung high they would let go and fly out and land on the soft, foot-churned dirt. It was as a swingset acrobat that Benny excelled all others. He flew through the air with no fear. He moved with grace and landed with poise.

One day Terra and her group (which was also my group by default, as was Benny's group) approached the swing sets, and Terra called the girl against whom the universe had conspired all four of her bad names.

At first the girl tried to answer and defend herself. She tried to call Terra names in return, but her words would not come out right, and she only managed to make herself look more foolish. Something inside the girl snapped. She stopped swinging and made a run at Terra. She swung both her fists and came close to hitting her, but Terra stepped aside and tripped her at just the right moment.

The girl fell down and laid there for a few seconds. Then she rolled and grabbed Terra's ankle. She yanked and Terra fell down beside her. They struggled back to their feet, and they were about to tear into each other (which would have been disastrous for the poor persecuted girl since Terra was a wonderful fighter), but somehow Benny got between them and held them apart.

"I'm gonna kill her," Terra yelled. "Let me go, you stupid $@# boy. I'm gonna kill her."

"No," Benny said.

"You ain't my daddy, Benny Carpenter, so don't you tell me what I can't do."

"I'm not telling you what you can't do. I'm telling you what I won't let you do."

The poor tortured girl clawed to get at Terra, but Benny

17

fixed his eyes on her and said "no," and it was as if her spirit left her. The girl just shrugged and walked away.

I saw the girl, Terra's torture object, years later. It was after I became a nurse. I was working in the emergency room at Springhill Hospital, where I still work, and someone brought her in on a drug overdose. We kept her from dying, but it wasn't because she was struggling to survive. She didn't care one way or the other. After we cleaned her out, we sent her to the psych ward, and I lost track of her after that.

SIX

After fifth grade we moved up to middle school, and Terra went from bad to worse.

I am perpetually perplexed by how naïve most adults are to the ways of adolescents. The average adult looks at the average sixth grader as a big child, a near innocent being. It goes double if the sixth grader happens to be their own offspring. Adults forget how they were at twelve, but working in an emergency room, I can't forget. I see a kid that age not as a big child but as a small adult, already full of all the desire, pride, and brutality of a grown person. Kids are sneaky and they hide well, but don't be fooled. They know much, especially stuff they're not supposed to know, especially if they go to school with someone like Terra.

Terra educated all of us. One of her mother's boyfriends kept a stack of men's magazines, and she read them all. She had begun to fall behind in her schoolwork, but she had a near-perfect memory for trash.

She was far and away the prettiest girl in the entire school. The boys heaped attention on her, and she reveled in every bit of it. She got active with the boys for the first time on our field trip to Montgomery. We boarded a tour bus before daylight, and she got on first. She dashed to get a back seat. The two cutest boys in class joined her, each on one side, and throughout the drive they, well, you know, experimented.

Benny and I sat near the front and talked. He knew what was happening, and though he did not speak of it, he showed pain in his expressions.

By seventh grade, Terra was all things to all boys, but an odd thing began to happen in her thoughts and feelings. While she craved the boys' attention, she began to despise the boys. She told me so.

When we went to cheerleader camp before eighth grade, we stayed at a hotel near the University of Alabama, two girls to a room, a bed for each girl. She and I roomed together, and she sneaked a boy into the room.

They got completely under the covers together. There was tossing and turning, and I looked away. I thought I knew what they were doing, but a few seconds later, the covers flew off, and I saw that he had a bloody nose. He was pulling her hair, and she was biting his arm.

I screamed, and our chaperone came from the adjoining room.

"What's going on in here? Hey, you get out of here! Who are you, anyway? Angel, who is this boy?"

The boy grabbed his shirt and ran out the door, and Terra sneered and said nothing.

Benny's love for her did not weaken during those years. If anything, it grew stronger. Each year on Valentine's Day he would bring her a valentine with a piece of candy inside.

She would say, "Why do you do this, you freak?"

He would say, "I don't know," and walk away.

She would remove the candy, eat it, and trash the card.

For most of those years, I stayed close to Terra for the entertainment, but eventually I wearied of her shenanigans. Then my care for her continued on its earliest basis—the inexplicable draw of her vulnerability.

SEVEN

Ninth grade came, and we moved up to the high school. Benny had been losing friends since seventh grade, and by the ninth I was one of his last two companions, the other being LuAnna McKinsey. As children, the outsiders he befriended had been eager to accept his friendship, but paradoxically, the fact that he could have been popular made him suspect. It made them think he might have been condescending. In the end, they rejected him too. Such was the nature of their self-loathing.

Most of his ex-friends gravitated to the youth subcultures of the eighties—comic books, D&D, heavy-metal, and drugs. LuAnna remained his friend only because she was the absolute bottom of the social barrel, and not even the metal-heads would have anything to do with her.

LuAnna came from the worst of all white trash social castes. She was scrawny and ugly in the face. Her dishwater blonde hair was always disheveled and sticky, and she wore the same set of clothes to school each day.

Her mother and father were fat, toothless, and always unemployed. They mostly just sat around, watched TV, and ate what they bought with food stamps. They lived in a trailer with several holes in the floor, and small dogs and cats ran in and out of them. The trailer, which I visited once and could never go back, stank like a dump, and LuAnna and her whole family had a bad smell about them.

A few weeks before the homecoming dance, Terra, whose power, especially with the boys, was as firm as Caeser's over Rome's army, led the class to play a joke. They would vote LuAnna into the homecoming court. Each class picked two homecoming maids, and Terra knew without a doubt that she would be one of them. She nominated LuAnna to fill the other slot and told everyone to vote for her. LuAnna's election to the court would be funny to everyone, but it would also keep Missy Daniels, the second prettiest girl in class and Terra's rival, off the football field, off the hood of a car, and out of the spotlight. Terra always had her ulterior motives, as if her obvious motives weren't bad enough.

Terra and LuAnna both won by landslides, and everyone but Benny had a good laugh. Even I laughed, I am ashamed to say, at the idea of ugly LuAnna McKinsey being paraded about on the hood of a fancy car, standing before the entire school during half-time at the homecoming game, and waving at the bleachers as the band played the school song.

Our homeroom teacher understood what had happened, and she broke the teachers' unwritten code of sanity, which roughly states: since you can't help without being punished for it, ignore everything.

At the weekly teachers' meeting, she told her coworkers what had happened and asked for donations. All the teachers chipped in, and they bought LuAnna a decent dress and made her an appointment for a makeover on the afternoon before the game.

LuAnna asked Benny to be her escort, and he told her it would be his honor. After that, I could tell by the way LuAnna talked that she had begun to convince herself that she had really won the place on the court, that just maybe people liked her as much as anyone else and that her life was about to change. She almost succeeded too, but when the big night rolled around, her delusions shattered when she and Benny walked onto the field and heard, mixed with the clapping, the sound of laughter.

She didn't cry, though. She hardened her face and took it. She walked with her head high and even managed to smile.

After the game LuAnna said she wasn't feeling well and wouldn't be able to attend the dance. Benny said he was sorry to hear it, and he and I went to the dance together. We danced with each other several times. We talked of our memories of things as far back as kindergarten, and I felt closer to him than I had ever felt to anyone, but for all our closeness, there was not then and never was anything but a friendship between us. Several times he glanced in Terra's direction, and I could tell he was trying to get up his nerve to ask her to dance.

When at last he went to her, I watched from the other side of the gym. He approached, smiled, and spoke. She glared, shook her head, and turned her back. His smile wilted. He turned and walked back to me, and we danced the rest of the night without talking. During slow songs, I held him close, and though he did not speak, I knew from the slow awkward way he moved that his feelings had been hurt badly. His weakness for her made me love him all the more, though. I would not have been able to articulate why back then, but I know now that it was because he was, for all his strength and strangeness, human.

The morning after the dance, I woke up and walked into

the kitchen. Mom and Dad were sitting at the table, and they weren't talking.

Dad whispered, "You tell her," and Mom rolled her eyes but accepted the duty.

"Angel, sit down," Mom said. "We've got to tell you something."

"What is it?" I asked as I began to imagine the worst, which was exactly what it turned out to be.

"You knew LuAnna McKinsey, right? Didn't you go to her house one time?"

"Yes."

Mom continued with the story, but she didn't have to. She had already used the past tense, and I knew what it meant. I only needed to know how she did it.

She had used her Mom's old pills.

I called Benny. He had already heard. Everyone in his trailer park was talking about it. His mother was at work, and he was by himself. I invited him to come over, and he rode his bicycle.

We sat in lawn chairs on the patio, and Benny said he didn't want to go on living.

"Because of LuAnna?" I asked. "Listen, she wouldn't want you to join her. She would tell you that if she could."

"I know," he said, "but it's not about her. It's about Terra. I don't understand why things have to be the way they are with her and me. Why is she the way she is?"

If I had thought hard enough, I probably could have explained why Terra was the way she was. She really wasn't so complicated. What I wanted to know was why Benny was the way he was.

"Why do you care about her so much?" I asked.

"I don't know. I don't even want to care about her."

"She's not worth it, you know. She's no good," I said.

"I know that," he said. "I know it with my mind, but I can't help what I feel. I can't help it, Angel. I know I'm stupid, but I can't help it."

EIGHT

The Sunday paper announced that LuAnna's funeral would be held on Monday afternoon at the same Baptist church that you and I passed by when we took our ride in the Cadillac.

Why don't you and I get back in our big, yellow Eldorado, and drive it to the church to participate in the events of the day? Come on, I've got the engine warmed up and the top down. An early October day in Alabama like this one is what a car like ours is made for.

We arrive early, but the church sanctuary is already full of people, and the parking lot is full of cars so we have to park down the road.

We enter the back of the church and notice that my classmates are sitting in one cluster, and the younger version of me is sitting between Terra and Benny near the center of the group.

Terra is crying. Most of the other girls are crying too. Suddenly they are all former close friends of LuAnna's. They were "like sisters with her. LuAnna was such a wonderful person. LuAnna was special. Why is it that it's always the good ones, like LuAnna, who die young? Wasn't she just beautiful at the homecoming game?"

Terra explains that she nominated LuAnna because she thought it would make her feel good about herself for a change. If she had only known how much everyone truly loved her, LuAnna wouldn't have done this. If only she could see this wonderful funeral.

These girls live for such contrived drama as this. They weep and hug one another, and they feel close to the center of something big. Yes, this is a big thing. Everybody is here. School is out for the afternoon, and everyone from the principal to the janitor is present.

Someone had rushed to get the homecoming photos developed, and several large photos of LuAnna in her fine dress adorn the sides of the casket.

Sitting on the front row is an elderly woman with bluish white hair, LuAnna's grandmother. She has used so much hairspray that her hair stands out six inches from her head in all directions. A fly is stuck in her hair, and it is fighting to get out. It is struggling to survive, thinking, if flies think, that it must be trapped in some thick spider web. Its motion is fierce and wild, but so bulky is her hair, so coagulated is the spray, and so oblivious is the woman that she does not feel it.

LuAnna's mother is sitting on the woman's right side. She is nearly motionless, her eyes focused on nothing. LuAnna's father sits to her mother's right, and his left arm is about her shoulders. He keeps dabbing his eyes with a handkerchief and shifting his weight from side to side. His thick beard and scraggly brown hair are wet.

After a song, the preacher walks to the pulpit and says we are gathered there in LuAnna's memory. As he reads her obit, the grating noise of repressed weeping fills the church. He eulogizes her as best as he can, but there really isn't much he can say.

Then he answers the question on everyone's mind: Can a person who committed suicide go to heaven? Yes, he informs us. There was one and only one sin that could not be forgiven, and it was not suicide. He is sure that LuAnna is with The Good Shepherd now, and the Shepherd is teaching His poor confused sheep what she failed to learn in life.

With all due respect, however, the preacher wants the young people to know how terrible a sin suicide is. Our own grief, he says, is a testimony to that fact. If any of us ever so much as think about suicide, we should call the preacher or some other adult in the community and tell them what we feel.

The preacher says a prayer, and the pianist and organist play Amazing Grace. The funeral director makes hand gestures, and his assistants wheel the coffin down the church's center aisle. The pallbearers follow, and they lift the coffin into the hearse. We file out the back of the church in a single line and go to our cars without lifting our voices above a whisper.

You and I ride at the very back of the procession to the cemetery. A county sheriff's deputy leads it in a patrol car. The preacher and his wife ride in the first passenger car. The hearse follows them, the pallbearers follow the hearse, LuAnna's family follows the pallbearers, and everyone else follows them in no prescribed order.

The deputy is thinking about breaking off his affair with the trash queen who works at the convenience store. There have been a couple of close calls with his wife.

The preacher and his wife are talking about what the church should do to reach out to the young people in the community so this doesn't happen again.

The pallbearers, riding in two cars, three to a car, are having nearly identical conversations about the weekend's Alabama-LSU game. Things haven't been the same at Alabama since the Bear died, and they probably never will be, they all agree.

LuAnna's family is not talking much.

The principal is talking to his wife about what would be the best way to prevent copycat suicides among the high school students, and he decides on having the school counselor work to locate high-risk students. Maybe they could all write essays, and the counselor could analyze the essays. His wife agrees it would be a good plan as she touches up her makeup by the reflection in the rear-view mirror.

Terra is riding with a group of eleventh and twelfth grade boys, and they are talking big to impress her. She may be a freshman, but she's already every high school boy's chief desire. Two of them have their arms around her to comfort her because she's so distressed over the loss of her good friend.

Benny and my younger self are riding with my mom. Mom and I are talking about how huge the crowd was for the funeral. Benny is not saying anything. He hasn't said much today, and my mom and I are worried about him.

You and I arrive at the cemetery and walk to the outside of the gathering at LuAnna's grave. Folks whisper in reverence until Brother Edwards raises his voice to call everyone in close. The circle tightens, and the preacher reads Psalm Twenty-Three. He asks us to bow our heads for a final word of prayer. He thanks God for LuAnna and what she meant to all of us. He asks for comfort for her family and friends. He says "Amen," and that concludes the official events of the day.

You and I get in the Cadillac and drive it back to Lott Road to the McRary intersection, pull over, and get some of that barbeque.

NINE

The following Wednesday the school counselor visited our homeroom. Our homeroom teacher yielded the lectern to her, they exchanged serious glances, and the counselor announced that she would like for us all to write an essay.

She said the essay would not be graded and that we could relax and write whatever we felt like writing. She wanted us to answer specific questions with our essays, and she wrote the questions on the board.

1. Are you happy? If so, why? If not, why not?
2. Do you feel loved? If so, by whom? If not, why do you believe people do not love you?
3. How do you feel about yourself?
4. How do you feel about life in general?
5. Do you get along with your family? If so, describe your family life. If not, what do you believe is wrong?
6. How do you feel about the recent loss of your classmate? Were you close to her? Have you ever thought about suicide?

The counselor assured us that our essays would be kept strictly confidential. She and she alone would see them, and by law (by law!) not even our teachers could look at what we wrote. She told us it was extremely important for us to be honest and hold nothing back. We could take as long as we wanted to write our essays.

Taking as long as we wanted meant cutting algebra class short. Ironically, our leading algebra student realized this first and communicated it to the rest of us by writing it on his desk and erasing it before he was caught. Those near him passed the word around in the same manner, but by the time it reached the far ends of the class, everyone else had thought of it anyway.

When we saw the last question, Terra and I glanced at each other and rolled our eyes. We knew what this was all about, and we knew the answers we should put down in order to avoid counseling sessions during study period. Study period was the best time of the day to write and exchange notes, and we could not miss it.

For me, avoiding the counselor was simple. I merely had to tell the truth. The idea of suicide frightened me, and I would never even consider it. My life was okay, and I had a pretty good family.

Terra lied about her family life. She said she had a good one when in reality she had none. Terra had been taking care of herself since she was old enough to walk. She saw her mom late at night, if at all, and she had seen her dad only once in her entire life.

A few days later, we figured out who had been selected for counseling. Nobody had to tell us. Three students started missing study period in rotation, and we just knew.

The first was an unattractive girl who was prone to dramatics. Her essay must have been a real outburst. Although we knew where she was going, she went the second mile and dropped big hints. "I've got issues, major issues, and I've just gotta get'em worked out, and I know I will."

The second was a metal-head who always wore black. He was a shoe-in no matter what he wrote.

Benny was the third. I asked him why he thought he got selected, and he said it was probably because he gave one word answers and short explanations.

I asked him why he did that. Surely he knew what the counselor was angling for. He said he knew, and that was why he kept his answers short. He didn't want to raise any red flags by saying too much, but he guessed his strategy backfired.

I asked him how he liked the counseling, and he said it was okay, and if he kept going he might eventually help the counselor straighten out her problems. We had a laugh at that, but then he turned serious. He said he didn't get anything out of the counselor's psychobabble, but he didn't mind going. It was interesting to try to figure yourself out. The counselor had him thinking about what he was going to do with his life.

I asked him what he was thinking about doing, and he said he didn't know. He was just thinking about it. Maybe he would go to college and study engineering. His math scores were good enough. Maybe he would go to trade school and become an air conditioning repairman. Maybe he would become a cop.

He asked what I wanted to do, and I told him I wanted to be a nurse. He asked me why, and I told him I liked the white uniforms. Nurses always looked so strong and pretty, and I wanted to be one.

After I talked to Benny, I asked Terra what she wanted to do, and she whispered it in my ear. My face turned red. I giggled, slapped her on the shoulder and said, "No way. Are you serious?"

"Yes, I'm serious."

TEN

Terra could not legally enter her chosen line of work, dancer (not ballet), until she turned eighteen, but she found the perfect place to train until then, the diner that had taken the place of the barbeque trailer at the corner of Lott and McCrary. As soon as she turned sixteen, not long after we entered tenth grade, she got a job there waiting tables.

There are two kinds of waitresses in the world. There is the kind that politely takes your order and serves your food, meeting all the obligations of the job. This kind might make friends with you and be a real friend to you if you frequent her restaurant often enough, but the friendship never crosses into the business of the customer, and the business never crosses into the friendship. This kind of waitress is a decent and honorable servant of the dining public.

Then there is the other kind. For lack of a better term I'll call her the "table harlot." Table harlotry must be an ancient profession, its roots going so far back into antiquity, who can say when it began? Was it with the maids who served ale to traveling merchants in medieval inns? Was it with the female slaves who served bread to the noblemen of Egypt? Was it with the Stone Age women who prepared and served meat for the men who brought it to the cave? I doubt anyone knows.

The table harlot is a flirt, a tease, and a seller of false hope. She pretends to like a man more than she really does.

Terra took to table harlotry like a bulldog takes to a fight with a poodle. A typical white trash man would come in for

31

supper, and she would work him like loose clay. She would exaggerate her smile upon seeing him. She would pat his shoulder when she asked for his order. When he would stand to leave, she would touch his arm, maybe give him a little pinch on the bicep.

Benny got a job at the grocery store across the street at about the same time Terra went to work at the diner. He became her regular customer, but she never practiced her table harlotry on him. She barely acknowledged his presence. She never so much as brushed against him when he sat on one of the stools by the counter. When he ordered, she spoke of nothing but food. As much as she could, she stayed on the end of the diner opposite from where he sat.

When Benny and I came in together, we would sit in a booth, and she would sit beside him to talk to me. That was as close as she would get to him, and then it was only to be able to look me directly in the face when she spoke.

Now, it could be argued that Benny's visiting the diner when Terra was working was completely out of line. If a flirty waitress practices a form of harlotry, a male customer who has an unwelcome affection for a waitress practices a form of extortion. He uses his power as a customer to wrench her attention and courtesy from her.

Indeed, if Benny had engaged in that kind of opportunism, he would have been entirely wrong. I would have lost all respect for him, and I would not be telling you this story. He did nothing of the sort. He never asked for anything but his food. He never tried to start a conversation with her. He never so much as looked her in the eyes when she was working, but he left generous tips and stacked his silverware and plates in such a way that gathering them would be easy for her after he left.

One afternoon during Christmas break, I stopped him in

the diner's parking lot and told him what I thought about his ridiculous love (I had my doubts that it was "love"— more like a mental illness) for Terra.

"Benny," I said, "she's one of my two best friends. You're the other one. I don't mean to bad-mouth her, but I don't trust her. She keeps me amused, but she never makes me feel completely at ease like you do. She's fun, and I love her, but she's not a good girl. I know it. You know it. Heck, *she* knows it. Why don't you forget about her and move on to someone worth your love?"

"There's just something about her…"

I interrupted him, "No, don't be stupid. There's nothing in Terra for you to love. She's totally depraved."

"I mostly agree with you," Benny said. "There's not a lot there, at least not for now, but there is a possibility something will be one day. There is something in her that is lovable, something either not spoiled, or if it is spoiled can be unspoiled somehow."

"You can't unspoil something," I said. "Once something is spoiled, it's spoiled."

"As a rule, that may be true," Benny said, "but every rule has an exception."

We were tenth graders. That was the deepest, most abstract conversation I had ever had. I would not have used an unusual word like "depraved" when I was that age, but it had been in our vocabulary lesson the week before the break, and it was still fresh on my mind.

ELEVEN

I met my first boyfriend in the summer between tenth and eleventh grades. I drifted from Terra and Benny for a while, and by doing so, I learned one of life's most important lessons. One should not let a romantic relationship ruin one's friendships.

Being something of a nerd, I had served as a balancing force in Terra's life, and losing me sent her farther down the road of depravity than she had ever been. Boys were old news by then, and she was looking for a new fascination. She found it at a party on the banks of the creek at the end of Lott Road.

She and four or five boys were partying hard one August night. They were laughing, drinking, and cranking a contradictory blend of music, rap-metal and outlaw-country, polar opposites culturally speaking, but both dear to the white trash kids of our time. One of the boys said there was something in his truck's glove compartment that he wanted to try and would anyone else like to try it with him?

Terra volunteered. He retrieved a bag of yellow pills. Exactly what they were Terra never knew. He gave her one. He took one and washed it down with a slug of beer. She did the same, and for a few minutes, she didn't feel a thing. Then it hit her all at once.

She felt a peaceful warmness in the center of her torso. The warmness spread, like a gentle wave, in all directions, and a few seconds later she felt like everything in the world was just fine. She felt comfort as if she had been a little girl, and her father, whoever he was, was holding her in his arms and telling her how pretty she was going to be when she grew up. She felt love as if she were in love, which she never had been. She felt happiness as if Alabama had just won the national championship and she was a Crimson Tide cheerleader.

A few minutes into the high her skin began to itch, and the next day she was constipated, but the itching was mild, and the constipation was remedied with a pink pill that she took before going to sleep. Such side effects were a small price to pay for such bliss.

That same summer, Benny increased his religious intensity, and I could not help comparing his zealousness to Terra's drug use. In part, it seemed like escapist behavior. He began to attend church services three times a week: Sunday morning, Sunday evening, and Wednesday evening. He helped his pastor with mission work at the local shelter for derelicts, recovering alcoholics, and drug addicts.

He lost himself in religious devotion, a thing I did not understand at the time, and he began to talk about the Bible every day. His religious fervor increased his isolation at school to the point that any other student would have been overwhelmingly lonely, but he managed to get by. He had his "church family" to take up the gaps in what he missed with his peers. At church, there was love for him in abundance. The only problem was that most of those who attended church were much older than Benny. He was their finest son and they appreciated the devotion they found in his young face, but they could not give him all the companionship he needed.

My summer romance ended not long after school started back, and Benny and I got close again. We ate lunch together every day. He would be so full of thought by the time lunch rolled around that he would burst into talk, and all I could do was listen and nod my head in agreement from time to time. His talk was usually religious in nature, and I did not understand most of it. I never gave religion much thought back then.

One day when we were munching our sandwiches, he asked me what was wrong with Terra.

"Do you mean in general or just now?"

"Just now, I guess."

"She's popping pills," I said, feeling very cool for rolling off a phrase like that, "started this summer."

"Are you serious?"

"Yeah, I'm serious. I would tell you to ask her yourself, but she wouldn't talk to you," I said, not intending any cruelty, just stating a fact we both knew.

"Does her mom know?"

I laughed. "Does her mom care?"

"Guess not," Benny said. "Is she hooked?"

"Yeah, totally. Doesn't take long, you know."

"I know. That's what they all say at the shelter. Maybe she should go to the shelter."

"Yeah, right. Like they could keep her there."

"No. I mean she should just go by and look at the people, you know, talk with them about how they got there. Why don't you figure out a way to get her to go?" he asked.

"Me? I can't get her to do anything she doesn't want to do."

"But you could think of something. Come on, it would be good for her. She's your friend."

"I'll think about it."

Our conversation took a turn in another direction, but a few minutes later, I figured out how I could get her to stop by the shelter, and I abruptly changed the subject back to Terra.

"Hey, I know," I said. "One night when she and I are hanging out, I'll tell her I've got to return something to you. What could you loan me? Well, I'll tell her that you're at the shelter, and that I have to stop there to give you whatever you loan me. Then I'll tell her I'm afraid to go in by myself, which happens to be true, and she will come in with me. Nothing to it."

TWELVE

Benny agreed to loan me one of his tapes of Squire Parsons, his favorite southern gospel singer. He would then agree to loan it to one of the shelter's residents. Since I would have to return the tape, I would meet him at the shelter with Terra

When Friday came, I asked Terra to go for a ride with me down Airport Boulevard to holler at guys, but I told her I had to make a stop at the shelter first to give the tape to Benny, which meant we would have to drive out of the way. She agreed without hesitation. She was agreeable to most anything at that time.

We pulled into the parking lot, and I got out of my car. She stayed in her seat, and I asked, "Aren't you coming?"

"I don't like seein' him. You know that."

"You won't have to see him. I don't want to go in here by myself. Come on."

She sighed. "Okay, then. I reckon I'll go."

As we walked through the parking lot it occurred to me that if the visit were going to last long enough to do Terra any good, I would have to communicate to Benny that he needed to stay away from her.

THIRTEEN

Let's take another ride in that yellow Eldorado, you and I, top up because it's nighttime and the air is chilly and damp. This vehicle is a mystical machine, you and I agree, as we break the laws of time and space to get a clearer vision of the people and places surrounding our story's two main characters. The only problem is that the little crack in the windshield from our trip back to the seventies has spread in all directions, and we're worried that the glass may break.

We turn onto U.S. Highway Ninety-Eight and drive toward downtown Mobile. We pass Terra and the teenage version of myself and drive beside them in the left lane of this newly widened road. They are talking and they don't even notice us beside them as we give them a good, long look.

We accelerate past them and arrive at the shelter just as Benny and his pastor get out of his pastor's car. We follow them inside, and the first thing we notice is the smell of the place. Its elements are body odor, cheap perfume, urine, air freshener, disinfectant, and something we can't describe. It is not a strong smell, but it is unique.

The residents are wandering about on a break from their chores, waiting for the preacher to come and lead them in worship. We remain silent and they do not notice us as we study them. We have become invisible.

We see a tall woman, so thin that her ribs show through the tee shirt she is wearing. Her hair is long and stringy and dyed black. She is trying to look younger than she is (forty-seven), but her attire and makeup make her look twenty years older. She smokes one cigarette after another, and her voice sounds rough like rock grinding upon rock. She is here to battle many addictions. Just name it, she's done it and would like to do it again. The fact that she's alive is something of a wonder. She looks mostly dead. If she were sitting still, we would swear she was a corpse, dug from a concentration camp's burial pit. Her most recent place of employment was the streets of Mobile where she sold herself and whatever else she could get her hands on to sell. She is infected with the new virus they've been talking about on TV, but that's the least of her worries. This woman is lost, as lost as a human being can be.

We see a big guy with big eyes. He radiates nervous energy in all directions. His head is clean bald, and his clothes are offensive to the eye, the latest in punk fashion. He wears black combat boots and leather bracelets with chrome spikes. He stares at people and invades their personal space. His voice is loud and his laugh is obnoxious. He is oblivious to most of his surroundings and clumsy in his movements. His armpits, though visibly sticky with white powdered deodorant, emit a foul stench. He rubs his hands together over and over again and sometimes he talks to himself. He is not a substance addict, but this is the place for him because there is no other place in the world for him. He is a misfit in every sense, a man born to exist on the outside of all societies.

At the coffee maker, waiting for the drip to stop, we see an aging hippie. His hair is longer and stringier than that belonging to the woman we encountered, but it is not dyed. Currents of gray and brown run down his back like those in a waterfall on a polluted river. He wears a moustache that may have once been of the handlebar variety, but it has fallen down now and hangs off both sides of his chin. His cheekbones stand out behind his thin skin, and there is a swirly tattoo on his forehead, which, he says, he can't remember getting. His voice is nasal and high-pitched, and he is constantly talking, making jokes that do not make sense to the other residents, but he finds them quite funny.

Also waiting for the coffee to stop dripping is a young woman of remarkable beauty. She has blonde hair and blue eyes and looks to be in her early thirties, but she is only twenty-two. She is wearing a long-sleeved shirt to hide the needle marks that run the length of her fore-arm. She is thinking about her three-year-old son who is in foster care for now, and she is hoping to complete the program so she can get him back. She is hoping the preacher will say something, anything to get her through the night because the craving is strong just now. She wishes the man with the long hair would just shut up so she could gather her thoughts, but he won't stop talking. Her face is angelically sweet, but she's done things that would make the hardest resident shudder to be in her presence. She bears a resemblance to Terra, a strong resemblance.

Sitting on a couch in the area outside the chapel is a woman with two black eyes. She is not an addict. She is not homeless. Her name is on the deed to a house in the suburbs, same as her husband's name, but she will not go there because that is where he beat her until she could not stand up. She knows she won't be here long, but she has no idea where she will go next. Oddly enough to her, she doesn't mind the company of the residents.

Sitting beside her is a handsome man wearing well-pressed clothes. His hair is neat and sprayed in place, and his face is clean-shaven. He is smoking a cigarette and holding it between two fingers in a casual manner that suggests he is completely at ease. His voice is smooth and mellow, and he is smiling, and upon first glance we assume he must be the shelter's director or perhaps a doctor on call to help one of the residents, but he is in fact just another addict. His first addiction is alcohol, and the depth of his addiction is far beyond that of the most shabbily dressed residents. His fourth wife made him understand how bad he was when she filed for divorce. His second addiction is gambling, and he has lost more than most people ever earn. They don't deal with gambling addiction in this place, but if they knew how badly this traveling salesman wanted to play cards right now, they would place him in a straight jacket. He is a true salesman, a man born to do nothing but sell for a living, and as he talks to the woman she feels that the tone of his voice is that of a man trying to sell her something. The woman likes talking to him, but she doesn't trust him.

Following her to the chapel is a black man with feminine mannerisms. He wears many pieces of cheap jewelry. Many gold and silver objects dangle from the holes in his ears. Many bracelets adorn his wrists. Many chains encircle his neck. He wears a tight white tee shirt and tight black pants. He is the king of friendliness, and he greets all present with great enthusiasm, even those who cannot speak English.

Talking to the black man is a Mexican man. He is doing his best to communicate something of a very serious matter, but it isn't working. This does not stop the black man from pretending to be interested.

Walking behind them is a middle-aged woman in

flashy, tacky clothes. She is as bedecked in jewelry as the black man, but her taste is not nearly as good as his. Her hips are large, and they sway in wide, graceless swoops as she walks. She wears heavy makeup and tries to be friendly to everyone, but something in her eyes says that she hates this place and everyone in it. If she could be anywhere else she would be.

We wander into the chapel and have a look around. The décor is simple and mostly wooden—no fancy silver and gold plated ornaments in this place. The simplicity of the setting suggests the simplicity of the message that will be preached here.

FOURTEEN

By that time I held a subconscious, unarticulated belief that things never "just work out" so I was completely shocked that night by how smoothly our plan went at first. We entered through the double doors at the front of the gray block building, and they swung shut behind us.

Terra immediately recognized one of the residents as a relative. The jewelry-clad woman who looked uncomfortable being there was Terra's mother's cousin, and when she saw Terra, her entire demeanor changed. She stood up straight and motioned Terra over for a hug. She and Terra smiled, hugged, and fell into conversation.

This gave me a chance to find Benny and tell him I had gotten her to come into the shelter. He thanked me, handed me the tape, and said he would steer clear of her because if she saw him she might decide to leave. He exited the fellowship area and went to the kitchen. Terra never saw him there that night.

Until time for the service to start, the residents mulled about, talking to one another. Terra joined them. She knew their kind, and she knew their language. What she had not learned of their kind in the trailer park, she had learned in the cafe. She conversed with the salesman, stroking his ego so as to make him feel thirty years younger. She talked to the hippie-looking fellow about rock'n'roll, and that being his one great subject of expertise, he could not have been more pleased. She talked with the skinny black-haired streetwalker about makeup, and the woman lit up like a light bulb, which seemed entirely out of character for her.

Terra spoke with the young woman who bore no small resemblance to herself. At first they seemed like old chums, birds of the same feather, but the young woman, who was taking her rehab program quite seriously, took a solemn tone with Terra.

"So, what brings you here? What do you do?" she asked.

"What do you mean?" Terra asked in reply.

"What do you use? What drug? Or do you drink?"

Terra spoke before she thought, "Pills sometimes, and when I drink, I like... Wait, I'm not a new resident here. I'm just here with my friend. I don't have a problem like the rest of the people..."

The blonde said nothing. She merely looked Terra in the eyes and explained her own reasons for being there.

Terra grew defensive. "Listen, I ain't got no @$%# problems!"

"It's okay," the young woman said, "but maybe you should be here."

"No, I should not be here!"

The young woman laughed. "Relax. I don't mean as a resident. I only mean maybe you should be here tonight for the chapel service. Brother Edwards is preaching. Of all the preachers that come here, he's my favorite. He tells it like it is."

"Like it is, huh? How is it?" Terra asked, relaxing and grinning.

"It's good," the girl said, returning a grin, "and it's time to go to the chapel. Come on."

In the gentlest way possible she took Terra by the arm and began to walk toward the chapel door. So gentle and natural was the blonde's invitation and tug that Terra went along without protest or a second thought. I followed, and the three of us sat together, I on Terra's left, the blonde on Terra's right.

Benny's pastor entered the chapel by a side door and walked along the aisles, greeting the residents with handshakes. They warmed up to him as he made conversation, and by the time the service commenced, everyone was in a good mood.

The service began with singing. One of the shelter workers, a middle-aged lady with graying hair, played the old upright piano in the corner of the chapel. Although the piano's wooden exterior was worn and chipped with use, its sound was good. She played the songs from the traditional hymnal, and although some of the tunes were hundreds of years old, they seemed fresh and vibrant. The residents got into the singing, and a feeling of excitement and expectancy spread around the room.

After the singing, the preacher stood and started speaking. Terra, who had always made a point of ignoring moralizing adults, sat upright and paid attention.

At the shelter, Brother Edwards preached with more tenderness than he used at church on Sundays. I guess the condition of the residents brought out the depths of his compassion. He spoke of the Hebrew children following Joshua out of the wilderness into the Promised Land. He applied the story to his listeners by encouraging us to move on to the best place in life, away from confusion and away from wandering to a spiritual home. He concluded by telling the parable of the Prodigal Son, filling in many details to express the emotional force of the story.

I glanced sideways at Terra when the preacher was finishing up, and tears were forming in her eyes. I was not a religious person at that time, and I was not particularly moved by the sermon, but I was glad to see my friend moved by it. I hoped it would be the start of something new for her.

The preacher asked the pianist to return to the piano, and when she began to play softly, he extended an invitation. He asked us to close our eyes and open our hearts. The invitation was like those extended at the end of a Billy Graham crusade. Those in attendance were asked to make a decision if they hadn't made one already and to make that decision public by coming forward.

A perplexed expression came to Terra's face, and it was clear that she was torn. I knew her well enough to understand her facial expressions. At first she looked sad, then hopeful that something good was about to happen. Then she began to resist it all. She pulled her emotions back and she stood in place, tightly gripping the pew in front of us, trembling and weeping a little. The invitation continued for a few minutes, and two or three of the residents went forward to pray at the altar.

Then it was all over. The music ended, and the preacher dismissed us. Terra was pale for a few seconds. Then she returned to her old self.

I have often thought that if Terra had chosen to go forward that night, her entire life would have gotten better, and by default Benny's would have too, but things didn't "just work out."

FIFTEEN

Three months into our senior year, Terra turned eighteen and quit school. She started dancing in a club downtown, and because she was young and pretty, she made enough money to lose the economic aspect of her white trash identity. She spent most of it on her habits, however, and she remained white trash economically, socially, and in every other way.

I did not turn eighteen until close to the end of the school year, but a little while after Terra started dancing, she sneaked me into the club through the back door. I did not like the place from the moment I entered. Even in the back, the smoke was thick enough to choke a horse. The place smelled of cheap beer, urine, and armpit sweat— almost like the shelter. I sat with my back to the wall so I could take it all in.

The club was a place of illusions and delusions. The dim lights created the illusions. The brightest lights in the place were those over the pool tables, and they sat at the farthest distance from the main stage. The lights close to the stage were colored— red, yellow, blue — and the colors rotated from one to another in combinations that communicated certain moods. The real reason for the dim and constantly changing lights, however, was to keep the customers from getting a clear view of the dancers.

Pardon what may be an offensive statement, but except for Terra, the set of dancers reminded me of a pack of dogs. One of the dancers had obviously had several children, at least one of them by C-section. She had also had an appendectomy, a gallbladder surgery, and a knife fight. Her face was not bad looking, but her stomach looked like a faded road map. She danced with a feather boa and kept it around her waist as much as possible, which I am sure the customers appreciated.

Another dancer was just plain fat. She had a bulging, round belly, thick thighs, an elephantine derriere, and a big round head. I didn't admire her chosen line of work, but one thing I couldn't help admiring was her guts to try to make her living that way. She had guts, lots and lots of guts.

There was a dancer with chicken legs, chicken lips, and a hairstyle that ran over the center of her head like a chicken's comb. When she danced, she looked like, well, a chicken.

One dancer looked more like a man than a woman, and I couldn't help thinking that at one time, it might have been a man—or maybe it still was. I couldn't tell for sure what it was or what it was trying to be.

There was a dancer who looked so old that I was surprised she was able to walk, much less dance. Instead of using the pole at the center of the stage as part of her routine, she used it to keep from falling down.

Another dancer was probably as old as she, but this other dancer had had so much plastic surgery that her ears were almost on top of her head.

Well, I could go on with the descriptions, but you get the idea. Dimness was their ally, and without it, they would have needed other jobs, except for Terra. Terra could have stood before a hundred fluorescent lights and looked just as pretty. When she came onto the stage, every man there stopped what he was doing. The pool players lowered their cues. The bartender stopped pouring beverages. The disc jockey let the music play without looking for the next song.

It was not a demonstration of virtue on her part, but she exercised more modesty than the other dancers. She showed less but made more money than all the rest combined. Terra's stage show was a contradiction. Her beauty was no illusion, but her persona was. She came off as a shy girl who needed to be saved from a bad life, and many men offered to be her savior. Terra was happy to take their money, but she did not accept their salvation.

It was in fact the customers who needed to be saved from her. Like I said, it was a place of delusion as well as illusion. The illusions of the club enabled the men to lie to themselves. Outside the club, Terra would have never so much as touched any of the men who watched her dance, but inside the club she kissed each one on the cheek after taking his money.

SIXTEEN

"I miss seeing her around," Benny said to me during lunch a couple of weeks after Terra dropped out of school.

"Well, now you can see all of her if you want," I said with a grin.

Benny did not smile. He was never a prude or a spoilsport, but what Terra was doing was something he could not laugh about. He frowned.

"I can't see her that way. I can only see her the way I saw her the first day of kindergarten," he said.

"Well, you should break your rose-colored glasses and see her as she is."

"Oh, I see her as she is," he said. "I see her as she is because I see myself as I am."

He paused. I did not understand what he meant, but his words struck me with overwhelming force and caused me to remember why I loved both of them so much. They were both so extreme and incomprehensible.

Though I loved them both and had a good relationship with both, I could not understand the way they related to each other. Relate to each other they did! Benny held as specific a place in Terra's mind as she held in his. Terra related to him with hatred, but she related to him nonetheless. Apathy would have been the opposite of hatred, and she was not apathetic toward him. She hated him, and that was something.

We graduated at the end of May, and Terra returned to attend the ceremony. She showed up at the football stadium driving a red Japanese sports car. She wore a conservative black dress that must have cost a fortune by itself. The rest of her attire must have cost another fortune. She strutted into the stadium as if to tell us all that she was not graduating and was glad about it; she was doing better than any of us.

Benny saw her enter the stadium, and thinking that perhaps she would treat him differently on such a special occasion, walked over to where she was standing and extended his hand for a shake. She looked at his hand as if it had been a dead fish and turned her back to him.

Without showing any emotion, he turned and walked back to the place where he had been standing. A few minutes later the ceremony officially began, and those of us who were graduating formed a line at the stadium entrance to march to our seats.

The band played. Someone made a speech. I think he was a farmer who had been elected to the state house, but I can't remember. The valedictorian spoke. I think she said something about building a better world, but I can't remember that either. The principal presented our diplomas, and one by one, we marched across the stage that stood on the fifty-yard line and received them. It felt like walking through a dream. We tossed our caps into the air, and that was that.

For a few minutes, we graduates hung around the stadium. Benny and I talked about what we were going to do.

"I'm going to trade-school to learn air conditioning and refrigeration," Benny said.

"You could go to college. You could do anything you want," I said.

"I know, but this is what I want. What about you?"

"I'm going to trade-school to become a nurse. Mom thinks I should go to college, but I'll make more money nursing than I would teaching or something like that. But never mind that, what about right now? What are you doing tonight?"

"I'm working," Benny said. "What about you?"

"I'm going out with Terra."

"Well then be careful," he said, "and keep an eye on her. Don't let her get hurt."

"Keep an eye on Terra? Ha!"

SEVENTEEN

That night I found myself, or more honestly, I put myself in a position to keep an eye on Terra most of the time. We stopped at her club, and her manager offered me a job as a waitress. I took the job. I did it for the money. I needed cash for nursing school, and the job paid well for unskilled labor. The drunks spent freely.

I never danced. I never even entertained the idea, but more than one customer entertained the idea. I got offers and invitations, but I refused them all. Terra, however, refused no reasonable offer. She didn't even refuse most of the unreasonable offers.

The real money in dancing was in the side business, the oldest profession. I noticed that it took two forms—the blunt, straightforward form, practiced mostly by the older, less attractive dancers, and the sly, subtle form, practiced mostly by the younger, better looking girls.

Terra practiced both forms. The straightforward form she practiced with one simple rule that kept her from getting a disease. The subtle form she practiced with no rules at all. She preyed on the vanity and vulnerability of lonely men, same as she had done at the diner. She made them believe that a pretty young thing found them attractive, and like oxen to the slaughter, they went right along.

I asked her if she weren't afraid to meet strange men in their homes or hotel rooms, and she said she was not afraid because she always carried a gun in her purse. Besides, she said, she could read the men pretty well, and she only did business with the men she was sure were not dangerous.

Not only did she have an instinct about danger, she could always tell which men had money and which didn't. There were the pretend rich, way over their heads in debt, who drove Corvettes, 300ZX's, and other status symbols. Their type wore hip clothes, shiny shoes, and slightly gaudy jewelry. They tipped big, and that just put them further in the financial hole. They were all about symbolism with little substance, and Terra never bothered much with them.

There were the obviously rich. Their cars were of European make, usually forest green, beige, or some other discreet color. Their attire was usually golf or sailboat related. They tipped well too, but Terra never bothered much with them either. Their kind moved from woman to woman with ease, and she could not get her claws deep into them.

Then there were those who had plenty of money but did not show it. Most of them had no sense of style and would not have known how to show it even if they had wanted to. Others of them were just stingy. All of their kind had something constricted in their personalities, something desperate, something determined but ultimately weak. For Terra, they were the ideal prey. Complicated, yes, but ideal.

For example, there was the Korean War vet who had spent most of his life running a feed store on the west side of the county. His store had never brought in a huge amount of money, but his wife had been tight with every cent. She had had a knack for property investment at a time when the population of the west side of the county was growing like kudzu, and her death left the man rich and bewildered.

After three beers at the club, which I served, he started

pouring his heart out to Terra about his wife, and Terra asked to see a photo of her. The photo he showed her was the faded black and white he had carried in the war. His wife had been beautiful in her late teens.

The next night, Terra danced at the club with her hair styled identically to the way the man's wife had styled her hair for that photo. The old man was taken with Terra, and he was taken *by* her. She took him for a long ride, and along the way she managed to get her hands on half of his wife's fortune, which she promptly spent.

At first I felt sorry for him, but eventually I realized that on some level he knew what was happening, and he loved the illusion. He was able to lie to himself and believe himself. Not only did I not feel sorry for him, after awhile, I began to despise him for being so pathetic. His "love" for Terra was nothing like Benny's love for her. Even if he felt great emotions for Terra, the old man was really just a pervert, a delusional old pervert.

Terra told many sad stories to her customers. She told about how growing up she never knew her real daddy. She told how her mother had pointed him out to her across a parking lot once when she was eight. She told how she ran to meet him as he was climbing into his pickup. She told how he laughed and told her, "Git on. I don't know you. I ain't your daddy." She told how he cranked his truck and spun out of the parking lot.

Of all her stories, that one was the saddest. Of all her stories, that one happened to be true.

EIGHTEEN

Benny and I attended the same technical school, but we had no classes together. Our classes were long, and we saw each other mostly on lunch and snack breaks.

In high school, Benny was isolated, but at trade school, he made two good friends. Kevin Kyle attended a Baptist church on the south end of the county, and he and Benny hit it off immediately. Frank Davis attended an Assembly of God church. Benny said he had disagreements with him, stuff I did not understand, but they got along marvelously well.

The three of them had devotions together most mornings, and on Saturdays when they could get off work (all three had jobs), they went fishing at Big Creek Lake, drove to the beach, or went deer hunting. Benny loved to hunt, something he had never had an opportunity to do growing up, and he bought his first hunting rifle at that time.

I did not fit in with them at first, but I was happy for Benny. Just having a couple of friends was a big step for him, and his overall disposition changed. He smiled more, and at times he seemed lighthearted and carefree.

When one of my fellow nursing students, Deloris Spears, was diagnosed with a potentially fatal kidney disorder, Benny, Kevin, and Frank took it upon themselves to organize some fundraisers for her. She had no insurance, and although the doctors would have treated her, she would have spent the rest of her life paying for it.

They planned a carwash and asked the students in all

the programs to participate. Most did, and since we had placed signs all over the community, lots of folks brought their cars to the event.

Benny and I worked on the same team, and we had a lot of fun. I liked sinking the sponges into the buckets of hot water. It felt good all the way up to my elbows. After lunch, we all got into a water fight with the buckets and hoses, but the afternoon sun dried us out in no time. We raised over three thousand dollars that day—not nearly enough, but that was just the beginning.

The boys placed milk jugs at convenience stores with pictures of Deloris and photocopied notes explaining her situation and encouraging the donation of pocket change. They raised two thousand dollars in three months, but it was not enough, and the girl's condition worsened. She needed a kidney transplant fast.

They organized a barbeque and got permission to hold a benefit singing at Frank's church. The barbeque and the singing brought in four thousand dollars, and it was almost enough.

They were getting close on the money, but what the girl really needed was a kidney donor. All three of the boys volunteered to donate and got examined, but none of them had the same blood type. Deloris found a compatible donor when her first cousin volunteered.

I was having lunch with Benny and his friends a week before the day of the surgery, and Benny said, "We need to do something for the girl that's giving her kidney."

"Yeah, let's find out about her," Kevin said. "I've got Deloris's number. I'll call and ask about her cousin."

Kevin went to use the pay phone at the convenience store next door to our school, and while he was away, we talked about what we could do.

"We could take her out to eat," Benny suggested.

Frank and I agreed that would be best—the simplest ideas usually are.

Kevin returned with the girl's name—Connie Spears—and her phone number.

"We want to take her out for supper," Frank said. "Go call her."

"Okay, I will," Kevin said.

He went away again, and when he returned, he had it all set up. He told us we would meet her at the seafood place on Azalea Road on Friday night.

When Friday night came, five of us went, but three of us ended up being fifth wheels. Kevin and Connie, they told us later, felt electricity the moment they met. They each knew they had met "the one."

Around that time, I got the feeling that Frank was taking an interest in me, and I took an interest in him too. There were no sparks or explosions for us, but we got along well.

The convergence of Kevin's, Frank's, and my circumstances made us feel bad for Benny for not having someone, and I insisted that Frank not spend less time with Benny. I could entertain myself, and I did not want Benny to slip back into his isolated state.

The transplant was a big success. The surgery went off without a hitch, and Deloris's body received the kidney without any signs of rejection. Deloris had missed too much school to return to class that semester, but when she returned the following semester, the entire school welcomed her back with a celebration.

At the celebration, Frank took it upon himself to try to comfort Benny about not having a girlfriend.

"Don't worry, when you meet the right one, you'll just know it," Frank said.

"Oh, I do know it," Benny said, smiling back at Frank. "I know it."

He patted Frank on the shoulder and walked away.

Frank turned to me. "That was strange. Do you know what he meant by that?"

"Yes, and you wouldn't want to know."

"It's not about whats-her-face that y'all went to school with, is it?"

I didn't answer.

An expression of frustration covered Frank's face. "What's his problem? To be so wise, he doesn't know when to quit."

My relationship with Frank did not last. Despite Frank's admonishing Benny that he would "just know it," Frank and I did not "just know it," and there was too little chemistry between us. We remained good friends, however, and we shared in the camaraderie that was prevalent on our campus.

The eighteen months that I spent at trade school were among the best of my life. Well, actually, that is only half true. I spent my days among friends, studying and preparing for a career. I spent my nights among leaches, working a depressing job that felt miserable.

As soon as I finished nursing school, I quit my job at the club and took a position at Springhill Hospital, the closest hospital to where we lived, working the graveyard shift in the emergency room.

NINETEEN

Hey, why don't we go for a ride in that yellow convertible again?

We are driving around in the early nineties, and we are planning to spy on Terra, Benny, and the younger me.

It's 4:30 a.m. It is dark, and the morning is still. Terra is just getting home to her apartment in West Mobile, and she's got a customer with her. The man wants Terra immediately, and Terra wants what his money is going to buy her immediately after he leaves. She takes her customer inside.

When he leaves, she follows him into the parking lot and gets into her car. She cranks it and drives off. We follow her out of the apartment complex, half a mile up the street, then down a side road in an old neighborhood. She stops in front of a large white house. An electric bulb glows beside the front door, and we notice that the house's paint is cracked and peeling.

Terra hurries to the door and knocks on it. A dog barks inside. A dark man opens the door. He does not look sleepy or disturbed in the least. Terra goes inside, and he closes the door behind her. A minute later, the door opens and she hurries back to her car. She holds her purse unusually close to her body now. She looks both ways as she walks.

She's got something in that purse, and she can't wait to get home to put it to use. Then it will be off to sleep for Terra.

We drive to the breakfast grill down the street and have some waffles, eggs, grits, and toast. We watch the sun rise as it shades the grill's plate glass windows pink.

At seven a.m., the younger version of myself, just getting off work, enters the grill and sits on one of the round stools by the bar. My younger self looks tired but fully awake. My younger self knows the waitress behind the counter. She exchanges smiles with her.

The waitress gives my younger self that tired sarcastic look that says, "What depressing lives we live, Angel, and for what, eh?" She takes her order. It is the same thing we just had.

When the waitress brings the food, my younger self tells the waitress a story about something that happened in the emergency room, and the waitress laughs but looks uncomfortable doing so, knowing that one should not laugh at human misery, even if it is self-inflicted.

At eight o'clock, my younger self leaves the grill. We follow close behind her as she drives to her apartment. We look into her rearview mirror and observe that my younger self has a look on her face that says the waitress's unvoiced question has struck a nerve. She looks as if she is doubting that her life has any purpose. We drive on as my younger self climbs the stairs to her second floor apartment to spend the better part of the day sleeping.

At 8:30, we pull in behind a white van and follow it. On its bumper is a sticker that reads, "Don't lose your Cool! (Call Morton's)." Beneath one of the rear windows is a phone number for Morton's Air Conditioning Service, Benny's employer. Benny is driving the van to his first call of the day.

We follow him to the interstate and then north to the Saraland exit. Benny takes the exit, turns right, and takes an immediate left onto Shelton Beach Road. He drives a quarter mile and turns down a street with large, overhanging live oak trees. The houses here are of an average size, and most of the people who live in them are part of the area's working middle class. They work in factories, schools, and shops all over the county. South Alabama is hot and humid most of the year, and when they come home, they want nothing more than a cool house.

Benny pulls into a driveway, and a lady who looks about seventy opens her front door. Her face is long and horse-like, and she is sweating. She is not smiling.

"The unit is out back," she says, "but if you need to come inside, use the side door. I just put new carpet in the dining room."

Benny looks puzzled about her statement, but he walks to the side door to enter the house.

"Ma'am, where is your thermostat?" he asks.

"Right down the hall," she says as she lights a long cigarette. "You can find it. You don't need me to show you."

Benny shakes his head and searches for the hall.

"Stay off that new carpet," the woman says. "I thought I told you already."

"Yes, sorry, ma'am."

"Well, I'm going back to bed now," the woman says. "Try not to make any noise."

"I will need you to sign the receipt," Benny says.

"I'm not signing it until the job is done and I'm feeling cold air blowing."

"But I will have to wake you," Benny says.

"You'd better not," the woman says.

"But..."

"Just leave the receipt on the table when you're done," she interrupts. "I'll sign it and mail it myself."

"But I have to follow..."

"Yeah, okay, you have to follow your regulations or whatever. Give me the @#%# piece of paper, and I'll sign it.

Just don't wake me up when you leave, and be sure to lock my door."

Benny adjusts the thermostat and goes out back to the air conditioner unit. There in the morning sun, he works. He skins a knuckle against the edge of a fuse box, but he holds his temper and continues to work. He rubs sweat from his brow, and the blood from his knuckle smears across the side of his face. He cannot see it. He only sees his work.

He spends two hours working, and then he leaves for his next job of the day. He stops for coffee at his favorite convenience store and exchanges pleasantries with the cashier. He keeps moving.

He arrives at his next job, a brick house in West Mobile and finds a note on the door telling him he can't do it today. He'll have to come back some other time when it is convenient.

He departs for job number three—an auto repair shop in the south end of the county. There he is greeted warmly and welcomed by the secretary. Benny had installed their air conditioner, and had worked on it several times.

She smiles at him, and her gaze lingers. "Good to see you," she says. "It always is. How have you been?"

"Been well," Benny says. "Can't complain."

"You can go on back," the secretary says as she picks up the desk phone. "I'd better grab this." When Benny's back is to her, her eyes follow him across the room and out the door to the garage.

Benny knows that if he asked her, the secretary would go out with him on a date, and he wishes he could. She seems like a kind person, always polite and smiling, the kind of girl he knows he needs to settle down with.

Benny enters the garage, and he and the mechanics

exchange greasy handshakes, and as Benny starts to work, one of the mechanics asks him if he needs any help. Benny turns down the offer, but he strikes up a conversation about air intake systems for fuel-injected engines. The mechanic likes this topic. It is one of the few things in this world that he knows all about, and he chatters away.

Benny finishes the job in an hour or two, and the mechanic signs. Benny's workday is over early, so he decides to go fishing.

He goes home and packs his gear into his truck and drives across Mobile Bay to the pier in Daphne. At sunset he drives home, back to the same trailer park where he grew up. He rents his own trailer now, but his mother lives in the trailer across the way, and he goes and talks to her before he settles in for the evening. As usual, she is glad to see him, but she is very tired, and he doesn't stay long.

At ten o'clock, he watches the evening news. At ten thirty, he switches off his TV and goes to sleep.

He is alone.

TWENTY

Sooner or later every woman's beauty breaks. My grandmother, a dark-haired woman with Cherokee Indian blood, kept her beauty until she was fifty-two years old. At fifty-one she was still turning heads. Men would flirt with her when she went shopping, but at fifty-two she was just another middle-aged lady, invisible to men.

My cousin Rita lost her beauty at seventeen. When she was sixteen, every man, didn't matter if they were nine or ninety, turned to watch her as she walked. She had so much spring in her step that her already womanly body seemed to bounce from one point to another. That interest from the men got her in trouble, as they say, and when she became a mom at seventeen, she lost it and never got it back.

Terra's beauty broke when she was thirty-one years old. It's amazing that it lasted that long considering her addictions, the hours spent in a smoky bar, and her apparent disregard for herself. After her beauty broke, she made less money dancing and much less money on the side. She could not wrap men around her fingers anymore unless they were both seriously drunk and seriously lonely. At thirty-two, she lost a tooth on the right side of her mouth. It was not that noticeable, really, but it was just noticeable enough to tell the world that not only was she not pretty, she was white trash through and through. She was washed up, hung out to dry, old news, litter on the highway of life.

At thirty-three she was beyond desperate. Her work really was work now, and she worked long hours just to survive and get a fix. She left her apartment and moved back into the trailer park down the street from Benny's trailer park.

One night on my way to work, I stopped at a gas station, and as I was pumping she pulled in across from me.

"Hey Angel," she said, her voice sounding raspy and old.

I could not conceal my sadness for her when I replied, "Hey Terra. How are you?"

"Good," she said, "just fine. Never been better." Then she laughed sarcastically.

I shook my head, and an idea came to me, "Terra, do you remember that shelter where Benny used to volunteer, the one we visited that night?"

She looked puzzled for a few seconds, then the light of remembrance flashed in her eyes. "Yeah, I remember that place. I sure do. Nice people."

"Would you consider, I mean, well... I mean, don't take this the wrong way, but if I talked with the director, maybe you would like to go there, and well... maybe you should consider going there..."

For a few seconds she reflected on the idea, and it seemed as if she were in the valley of decision. A look of pain and of humility came to her face. Something inside her said "yes," but before words came out of her mouth, something else inside her must have spoken louder because once again, she made the wrong choice.

A sneaky expression, very faint — barely perceptible — crossed her features for a split second. Then she smiled. "I don't need no shelter for drunks and drugheads. I'm fine really, but you mention Benny. How is he doing?"

These were the most shocking words I had ever heard Terra say. She had actually asked about Benny. I could not believe it. I forgot the sneaky expression and everything else.

I spoke without thinking. "He's doing great. He works for Morton's, repairing air conditioners. He lives in the trailer across from his mom's."

She smiled and raised an eyebrow. Then she changed the subject.

I drove to work. That night started out slow.

TWENTY-ONE

The events I am about to relate, I did not see. Terra confessed them to me, and for once I trust her every word.

After seeing me at the gas station, Terra drove to Benny's trailer park and located his trailer. She climbed the block steps and knocked on his door.

"Who is it?" she heard him mumble out of his sleep.

"It's me, Terra."

"Terra Peoples?" he asked in a fully conscious, fully awake, excited voice.

"Yes, of course. It's been a long time and I was in the neighborhood. Am I waking you up?"

She heard Benny moving quickly about the trailer. "It's okay. Just a second. I've got to find something to wear. My trailer's a mess. Don't look around when you come in."

"It's okay," Terra said. "I'm just glad to get to see you."

Benny opened the door. If he suspected anything at all, he did not show it on his face. He wore an expression of complete trust and gratitude.

"It's good to see you," he said. "Come inside. Can I get you something to eat? What about to drink? Are you thirsty?"

"No, but maybe I could give you something," Terra said through a slight grin. She sat on his couch, crossed her legs, and pulled her skirt to one side, revealing her right thigh. She looked around the room—nice décor for the trailer park. Like any successful white trash man, Benny had his hunting rifles prominently displayed. A guitar stood in the corner next to an amplifier. Down the hall to the bedroom his fishing gear hung on racks, and there was a lot of it. Terra did some quick calculating. She could get at least two thousand dollars for it all, probably much more.

"I'm sorry, what? I don't catch your meaning," Benny said.

She leaned to her left and hiked the skirt up a little higher.

"Oh, you know what I mean. You've always wanted me. Well, here I am."

"Oh, that. No. You don't understand. That's not the way I want you. I want..."

"Oh, put a lid on it. You want what every man wants. So let's talk. I've got my wants too, you know. Right now I want some money. You've got money, which I want, and I've got what you want." She smiled wide.

"You really don't understand, do you? You've never understood."

"I understand, alright, and I'm not waiting much longer. What's it going to be?"

"I don't want you that way. I..." Benny stopped short of finishing his sentence.

"You what?"

"I... I..." he stuttered.

Terra reached into her purse, pulled out her pistol, cocked it, and pointed it at Benny.

She laughed. "Say it. You what? I haven't got all night."

Benny tried to finish his sentence, but before he could get the words out, Terra said, "Oh, forget it."

She shot him. The bullet pierced his chest and exited just beneath his right shoulder blade.

Benny looked down and saw blood drip. He touched it with his fingers. An expression of puzzlement came to his face. Then a smile.

Then for the first and last time before he died, Benny

said to Terra, "I love you."

He fell flat on his face.

Suddenly Terra lost interest in robbing his trailer, and her craving for a high left her. She could not have explained then what she felt. She did not believe and could not let herself believe that Benny really loved her. Love did not really exist. Of course it didn't. If indeed he meant what he said, knowing that she had just murdered him, fully meant it, fully aware of what had just happened, well then that would mean... No, she could not accept that. Love did not exist. It just didn't.

She had to keep him alive. The only way she could walk away from what had just happened was to keep him alive.

She did not know that it was too late. Benny was already dead.

She picked up his phone and dialed 911. She said an accident had happened. They should send an ambulance without delay. She had heard the gunshot and had entered the trailer and saw him lying there. The man was in the living room. Sorry no more details. She had to go. They should hurry. Hurry.

She ran out of the trailer and got in her car. No one was stirring about so apparently no one had heard the gunshot, not that a gunshot would have been a big deal in that neighborhood.

She drove out of the trailer park. A mile up Lott Road, she parked in front of a convenience store.

When the ambulance came by the second time, she pulled in behind it and followed at a great distance. The ambulance drove straight to Springhill Hospital.

The driver had radioed ahead. We had prepped the operating room, and we were waiting for the unidentified male.

When I saw his face my knees went weak. I nearly

passed out, but I managed to stay on my feet. I swallowed hard several times, and tears dripped from my eyes. There were two doctors and five or six nurses. I could have excused myself, but something in me would not allow that. I was in that hospital in that emergency room for a reason. I felt it so strongly that I thought it might have been the sole purpose of my existence, that everything that had happened in my life until then had been preparation for this one night.

"Get him on the table," Dr. Abramson yelled.

A nurse and an orderly lifted his body from the stretcher and placed it on the table. I covered my mouth. For thirteen years I had been working in the E.R., and I knew what dead looked like, and Benny was dead. He was not "clinically dead," which means "almost dead." He was not "brain dead," which means "as good as dead." No. Benny Carpenter was dead, absolutely dead.

"Get the cardio monitor on him," Dr. Abramson said.

I placed the sensors on his chest, forearms, and forehead. I flipped the switch. Nothing. No heartbeat.

"He's dead," I said.

"He's lost blood," Dr. Abramson said. "Could be some low level fibrillation the monitor wouldn't pick up. I'm going to shock him."

He reached for the paddles. He placed them on Benny's chest. He turned to the nurse at the switch. Ready... one... two... three...

Benny sat straight up. His eyes opened. Without searching the room, he looked straight to the door, which was slightly ajar. In the dimness of the hall, he saw two blue eyes peering back at him through the opening. My eyes followed his. I saw her eyes, and I knew that she had done this. Their eyes locked.

In a calm, clear, firm voice, he said, "I **SAID** I love you!" Then he lost consciousness.

Then she left.

We worked on him. The doctors cut him and sewed him. The nurses ran blood into his veins. We gave him medicine. For fourteen solid hours we worked on him. Seven hours after I should have been home in bed, I was still there, doing what I could do. I left only after his condition stabilized—critical but stable.

He lay in a coma, but he was alive. Benny Carpenter was alive.

TWENTY-TWO

As I pulled my car into its usual parking space at my apartment complex, I saw Terra sitting in a car in the space next to mine. Her sleeping patterns were as irregular as mine, and it was obvious that she had neither slept nor needed sleep. She got out of her car as I was opening my car's door.

"Well?" she asked.

"He's alive," I said.

"Yeah, I knew he would be."

For the first time in my life I spoke to her as an enemy, and I used the three worst words I knew to call a female.

She looked down for a few seconds. When she looked up, tears were dripping from her eyes.

"Yes," she said.

"As soon as I can get to the phone, I'm going to call the police and turn you in. What are you going to do about that? Going to shoot me too?"

"I knew you would, and I deserve it. Can I wait inside for them to come? I've thrown my gun away. You got nothing to worry about."

"Okay, why not? In fact, you could surrender. They might go easier on you."

"I am surrendered, but I can't call the police. I would. It's the right thing to do, but for Benny's sake, I can't."

We climbed the steps to my apartment, and I opened the door.

"What do you mean?" I asked as I switched on the living room light and picked up the phone.

"Look, I deserve prison. I deserve to die. They still execute people in Alabama, don't they? Well, I deserve that. No doubt about it, but if I'm gone, Benny won't have me to love."

I sat down for a second. I held the phone, and I thought very hard. After awhile, I set it back on the receiver.

"I can't turn you in," I said, "not without his permission. Your fate belongs to him. If he dies, I most definitely will turn you in, but if he lives, well, whatever happens to you will be his choice."

"He'll live," she said.

"What makes you so sure?"

"Didn't you hear him?"

"Yes," I said.

"Don't you know, then?"

I sighed. "Yes, I know. He will live. Go to him."

She went.

TWENTY-THREE

I slept that afternoon and returned to the hospital for the evening shift. I arrived early and stopped at the ICU waiting room. Benny's mother was there. As always, she was quiet. Brother Edwards and his wife were there.

"Terra Peoples is with him right now," Brother Edwards said. "You're a friend of hers, aren't you, Angel?"

I grunted. At that point, I would have said *no*—no forever, but there were Benny's feelings toward her, and his feelings would determine my feelings.

I went inside the unit. Benny was still unconscious, but Terra was holding his hand, and in his deep sleep, he was squeezing her hand.

"He loves me," she said.

The Terra I had known my entire life was gone. Where she had gone, I did not know. Maybe when Benny died, the old Terra died too. This Terra was a different person.

"What has happened to you?" I asked.

"I don't know," she said, "but his love won."

"Love won?" I mused out loud.

"Angel, remember when we were kids, and we used to build castles in the sandbox on the playground? Remember how sometimes a big storm would come at night and the next day the castles would be gone? The sand would be smooth like a beach, all clean and new looking, like children had never played there at all.

"His love is like one of those storms," she said, "a million times bigger than the castles of my fear. It makes me clean. My fear lost. His love won."

"How long are you going to stay here?" I asked.

"Until he comes back. It won't be long. He's resting for now. Just resting."

On the third day after Benny Carpenter died, he opened his eyes and looked around the room. I was there at the time. I saw it.

Terra was there. Benny reached up and pulled her face down close to his and kissed her lips.

"I love you," he said.

"I know," she said. "I love you too, but I deserve to die for what I did. Do you want me to turn myself in? I will if you want."

Benny laughed, and his laugh was so big and warm and pure that it filled the room with an almost tangible feeling of joy.

"Shhh, don't be silly," he said. "You know better. No more to say about that." He pressed his index finger against her lips and whispered, "Shhh."

The police inquired, but Benny said that the wound was self-inflicted. "It happened under my own power," as he put it.

TWENTY-FOUR

She was his then, but since she had conquered his heart long before he had conquered hers, he said he wanted to start at the beginning. He told her to go home and get some rest, and I gave her some money to buy some food.

She told me to call her if anything came up, and I promised I would. In less than a week, something did come up—Benny. He left the hospital. The doctors were awed by the speed of his recovery, but they all agreed it was time for him to go.

"I'll call Terra," I said as he gathered the cards and flowers the people of his church had sent.

"Yes, call her," he said, "I would like to meet her."

He said "meet her" as if it were for the first time.

"Where do you want her to meet you? Your trailer or her apartment?"

He paused, turned his head, and looked out the window. "Actually, neither place. I've got a better idea."

He told me, and I laughed.

"You want to come too?" he asked.

I started to say "no," but I couldn't. I said, "Yeah, I'll come along. Why not? I'm just getting off work so I'll drop you off at your trailer and go pick her up. You can meet us there."

I went to her apartment and told her to get ready, that Benny wanted to see her, and immediately I noticed something that made my jaw drop. Some of her beauty had returned.

I don't know how much time passed, but awhile later I heard her snapping her fingers and saying, "Angel, hello. Angel, come back. Hey, stop drifting. How do I look?"

"You look great," I said. "Hurry, I want us to be there first."

TWENTY-FIVE

Terra and I walked across the playground. It seemed smaller now. A few more swing sets and sliding boards had been added, but the sandbox was where it had always been. We noticed a yellow bucket and a red shovel half buried in the sand, and we kneeled to dig them out.

Suddenly, as if he had materialized from the air, Benny was standing behind us. I sensed him there before I saw him, a gentle presence. I turned to look at him. The sun silhouetted his body, and for a moment he appeared to glow.

"If he grabs me this time," Terra said, "just let him."

We laughed. I hugged them both and told them I would be going.

TWENTY-SIX

You look like you're ready for one last ride in the Caddy. Hop in and buckle up tight. I'm not slowing down this time.

The moment they are alone together, we drive by, but instead of two thirty-three year olds, we see two five year olds, a brown-haired boy and a blonde-haired girl. The girl's smile works perfectly.

"When is it?" you ask as you rub your eyes. "Are we back in the seventies?"

"Yes, but not exactly," I tell you. "Time is blowing away."

We circle the school, and as we pass back by the playground we see that the children have grown. They are eight years old, and the playground has become a parking lot. Terra is crying because the man she was just told was her father is in his truck and peeling away.

But her friend from school, Benny, is there. When her father's truck disappears, he waves at the empty road then swings his hand down as if to say, "Goodbye and good riddance. Who needs you anyway?" Terra giggles and nods.

We circle again, and the playground is a fishing pier. Benny is sitting at the end of it. He is alone. We search his face for the deep pain of loneliness we have seen in the past, but it isn't there. Terra is walking down the pier, approaching him from behind. She's holding a rod and a bucket of bait. When he hears her footsteps, he looks up. She pats him on the shoulder, sits down beside him, and casts her line.

On the next pass, they are in their late thirties. Terra has a new tooth, but it matches the others so perfectly that we cannot tell which one it is. All of her beauty has returned, and we are startled by what we see. She is so beautiful that the sensation we experience is almost painful. The expression on Benny's face says he feels what we feel. He feels that he is the honored one. Her love is his joy. She and Benny are taking their children to the playground for the first time.

On our last pass, it is the present. I have just walked away, and there they stand.

"Let's go swing on the swing set," Benny says.

"Okay," Terra says.

A WAR STORY

Ray Fairchild: Down a dirt road is where we live, a red dirt road that turns off another red dirt road. Just two families live down here, the Boises and the Fairchilds. For years the only strangers we let down here were Brother Edwards and his wife to pick up the children on their church van.

We ran businesses, you see, and we couldn't have strangers nosing around. We had to be our own plumbers, carpenters, police, and even grave diggers. What kind of business, you ask, would we want nobody to know about? Call it specialty farming. I'm Ray Fairchild, and I'll be telling the Fairchild side of the story.

We kept bulldogs— all of us did. As far as I'm concerned the story starts with a bulldog.

Pete Boise: I'm Pete Boise, and I'll be telling the Boise side. I say it started when Junior Fairchild bought eight fighting roosters. We had too much going on as it was. We didn't need roosters on top of it, but he just had to have'em. So he built eight little rooster pens and eight little rooster houses and filled'em with eight gamecocks. Now it is true that my bulldog barked at them roosters, but they were invading his space. He had been there a long time before them. Like Ray said, we had all kept dogs for years. You can't just up and bring in a yard full of roosters and expect a dog to just lay still and be quiet.

Ray Fairchild: A man ought to have the right to buy what he wants and keep it on his own property without his neighbor's dog terrifying it to the edge of death, but we've agreed not to argue. Here's what happened. Bose Boise's sons each had a dog, and Pete's was crazy. I was scared of that dog. We all were, even Pete. When daddy bought his roosters, that dog wouldn't leave'em alone. For two days he spent his every waking minute smelling around their pens and barking at'em. Daddy figured he'd calm down and get used to'em, but he didn't. So Daddy told me to shoot that dog, and I'll admit that I did. I shot Pete's bulldog, Tiger.

Pete Boise: Tiger was a good dog. I wasn't afraid of him, well, at least not most of the time. He did get in a spell every now and then, but only when he was provoked, and when the roosters came, that provoked him. Then one night we heard a shot— figured one of the Fairchilds shot a deer. Next day, Tiger wasn't around. Now that wouldn't have been too unusual. Tiger would go huntin' down in the swamp, same as any dog. But after four days, he didn't come back, and we couldn't forget that shot.

Ray Fairchild: So one of you put rock salt in Daddy's rooster pens, didn't you?

Pete Boise: Yes, we said we're telling the truth now, so yes. But it wasn't just one of us. Me and both my brothers killed them roosters. Like we always said, blood for blood. Y'all killed my dog. We killed your roosters.

Ray Fairchild: Yeah, well, fair enough. So all of daddy's roosters were dead by noon. And then it was time we had a family meeting. You'll be wanting to know about my family so I'll tell you about us. First of all, there's Daddy. His name is Walsh Fairchild, but everybody calls him Junior, which doesn't make a whole lot of sense since Daddy's daddy's name was Crawford Fairchild. Daddy is a medium size man with a potbelly that fits his age, fifty-eight. His hair is still mostly red with a blonde patch in the front and gray coming in on the sides. His eyes are blue. He chews plug tobacco, and he smells like it— which is not to say that he smells bad, especially if you like tobacco.

Daddy is the toughest human being that ever walked the face of the earth. He loves a good fight, and that's why he got them fightin' roosters.

There's Mama. Her name is Helena. She was a Humphreys before she married. Now I don't mean to talk bad about my own mama, but she's too fat. She don't do much of anything, but she has an opinion about every-thing, and she's a smart woman, and her opinions are mostly right.

There's my sister, Calette. She started her family when she was fifteen— had twin boys, Ronnie and Donnie. They're eighteen. Ronnie has a three-year-old little girl named Lena that his girlfriend turned over to him to raise.

There's my brother Enton. He's thirty and married to Tancey, who used to be a Maples. They have three kids: Tanya, 10; Jimmy, 8; and Dan, 7.

I'm thirty-four and a bachelor. I've had lots and lots of girl-friends but no weddings and as far as I know, no children.

Pete Boise: I'll tell you about us Boises. Mama's dead. Daddy's name is Bose. I grant you that Junior Fairchild is tough, pound for pound, but my daddy is a big man, twice the size of Junior Fairchild, and in a fight, I think he'd win.

Ray Fairchild: That's your opinion.

Pete Boise: Yes, it is my opinion. My daddy's hair is white, and he wears a moustache. There's my younger brothers, Bo and Mike. Everybody calls Mike "Stump." That's 'cause he's short, round, and hard as wood. I've got two sisters, but only my older sister, Kate, lives here. She's a strong woman, and her husband, Maurice, is a skinny fellow who does what she tells him to do. Kate and Maurice have two children— Malisha and Tyrone.

Ray Fairchild: And that's all of us that lived down the dirt road— two families, not related but best friends all around.

Pete Boise: Right, but go on about y'all's family meeting.

Ray Fairchild: Oh yeah, the family meeting. We sent the kids in a bedroom to play and sat in the living room. Mama sat on the couch and Daddy sat beside her. Mama didn't say anything at first. She just sat there raising and lowering her eyebrows. She would raise her right eyebrow almost up to her hairline and lower her left eyebrow down even with the bridge of her nose. Then she'd raise the left one and drop the right one. Mama's got thick hair, dyed black, and dyed eyebrows and fair skin. Watching all that was sort of like entertainment.

Then she finally spoke, "We're not going to do anything immediately. We're going to pretend nothing happened. We'll throw the roosters down in the gulley, take down their pens, and let it all slide. Then in about a month, we hit'em. We'll cut their weed. Until then, we'll be friends, and after we hit'em, we'll be friends again.

"That'll be fair. Money for money. Them roosters were an

investment. Donnie would do the best job of it."

Donnie smiled when Mama said that. He never did have too much sense. I hate to admit such a thing about my own mama, but that's the reason she picked him. If anybody had to get shot, it would be best for the family if it were Donnie.

"Donnie can run faster than any of us," she said. "He's the best one— better if just one of us went, better on a moonlit night."

Daddy said, "Yeah, babe, good idea and until then we'll act dumb about them roosters. I found the rock salt, but when I see Bose, I'll say I reckon them roosters took bird flu. I heard about bird flu on the news. They'll think they got away with it, and they'll never know what hit'em when Donnie chops their crops."

I told them they had good ideas, and we all agreed to act natural. The meeting was on a Saturday night. After it was over, the women started getting the children's clothes ready for Sunday School.

The next morning, Brother and Sister Edwards came and picked up the children. I walked with them out in front of the house. When the van stopped, Brother Edwards said, "Ray, we'd sure love to see you in church. Why don't you come to the service?"

I said, "Yeah, maybe sometime— too much going on right now.""

"Ray, I don't ever see y'all doing much of anything down here," he said.

Now ordinarily I would be offended at somebody saying something like that, but Brother Edwards has a wide face that says he's your friend and a smile that lets you know when he's kidding.

I smiled and waved goodbye to the children.

Pete Boise: Maurice took the kids out to meet the van, and he told us how polite Ray acted, like they didn't suspect we had done anything. We were sure we had gotten away with killing the roosters and especially sure the next morning when Junior came over to sip coffee with Daddy on the front porch, and as he sat there he said how he'd heard about the bird flu on TV and thought it was a shame that his roosters taken it and maybe he should whip the man he got'em from for selling him sick birds.

Daddy told him not to whip him, that maybe Junior's roosters had caught the bird flu from a bluebird or a quail that flew by. There was no way to tell. After Junior left, Daddy came inside and told us what was said, and we all had us a good laugh.

We didn't think anything else about it until a month later, just about the time our crop was ready for cutting. Me and Stump walked our trail into the swamp and all but a little of our crop was gone. We went back and told the family about it, and Kate and Daddy said they wanted to see for themselves. They followed us down there. We showed'em, and Stump said, "I reckon the agents found it."

"It wasn't agents," Kate said. "They'd have come in the middle of the day and made a big deal about it. They would have had it on the evening news so as to show the community how good a job they were doing. It wasn't agents. It was somebody else. So what we need to do is look around these woods and see if they left any evidence behind."

Mud don't hold tracks, and neither does the straw and leaves on the dry places, but we did find a shoeprint in an odd spot. There was the reverse of a track on top of a stump. It was a tennis shoe print, where the mud had come off somebody's shoe— just one print.

"What about the Fairchild's crop?" Kate asked.

"They got some of it but not much of it," Stump said.

"Let's don't say anything when we first get back," Kate said. "Let me have a look at a couple of things."

So we went back and went inside Daddy's house. Kate went over to the Fairchilds on the excuse of wanting to talk to Calette.

After she got back, she told us what happened. Calette told her to come inside, and Kate looked around real close at everybody's shoes. Donnie was asleep on the couch, and his shoes were off. His socks had mud on them, and that was a clue, but she figured it out when he rolled over and his hands were stained green and cut up.

Kate told Calette she needed to go to the bathroom and she pretended to trip on Donnie's shoes as she walked past the couch. She rolled one of them over, and sure enough, the bottom of it matched the print on the stump. She talked a little more with Calette when she came back from the bathroom, and then she came back to Daddy's to tell us what she'd found.

"You don't suppose they knew about us killing their roosters?" Bo asked.

"Could be," Daddy said, "but Donnie is not real smart. He might have been thinking he'd get away with stealing our crop. We'll show him, though. We won't do it down here, though. In a few weeks when he goes to town, we'll get him good. He'll think it was muggers, but it will be you three with your faces covered.

"If it was just him, that'll be fair, and if it was all of them Fairchilds in on it, it'll still be fair. Donnie will pay for what they all did, and they'll all feel bad for him. Meanwhile we'd better tell 'em what happened and act like we don't know who did it.

Ray Fairchild: And feel bad, we did. It happened three weeks later. Donnie used his share of what we got for the Boise's weed to buy a truck, a blue Ford, as pretty as any truck you ever saw. He drove it proudly and spent Friday nights cruising around the parking lot of the grocery store in Semmes. When he stopped at the gas station on the corner of McRary and Highway Ninety-eight to use the bathroom, some men in ski masks got out of a truck and went in behind him. The clerk saw them and called the Law, but by the time the Law got there, they were gone, and my brother was almost dead. His truck, which they'd poured gasoline on, was burning.

An ambulance came and took Donnie to Springhill Hospital. A girl I knew from high school by the name of Angel Bonsecour was on duty at the time. She said what they did to my brother was the worst looking thing she'd ever seen. She said the men had stomped every square inch of his body.

He was bleedin' and bruised so bad that we didn't recognize him when we got there. We tried to talk to him, to ask him who'd done it, but he wasn't awake.

That's when Mama called another family meeting—right there in the waiting room of the hospital. She sat for a few minutes, raising and lowering her eyebrows.

Then she spoke slowly, "Did y'all see the way Kate was looking around all suspicious when she came to our house on the day after Donnie stole their weed? It was a little thing she was doing, and I barely noticed. I couldn't be sure then, thought it might have been nothing, but I'm sure now that she was looking at our feet. She saw the mud on Donnie's shoes. Bose's boys did this. I know it. I just know it."

"And we'll git'em for it," Daddy said. "If Kate thinks she's

Sherlock, let's see if she sees it coming. We'll burn down Kate and Maurice's trailer. They'll run out coughin' and cussin', and then she won't feel so big. That'll be payback for Donnie and the first thing we tell him about when he comes to.

"Ray, you do it. Go right now. Park off the road on the south side and go in on the swamp side of the property. None of our vehicles are at our place so they think we're all here. They burned Donnie's truck so this will be fighting fire with fire— which is fair.

Just as I was leaving, Brother and Sister Edwards came into the hospital waiting room. One of the police had told'em what happened. They were crying because they knew Donnie. He had gone on the van to church when he was a boy.

Pete Boise: About midnight, we were all in bed. We had taught Donnie a good lesson, and we were sleepin' well. Bo's window faces to the end of Kate and Maurice's trailer. Bo woke up in the middle of the night and ran down the hall hollerin' that Kate's trailer was on fire. We ran outside just as Kate ran out the front door of her trailer. She was holdin' Tyrone and coughin'. Maurice followed.

"Malisha," Kate screamed. She started to go back in, but Stump grabbed her.

"Let Maurice go," he said.

Maurice nodded and went. He came back a few seconds later, coughin' and wheezin' like he was going to die and cryin', "Her bed was on fire. Her bed was on fire."

He was holding a bundle in his arms. It was Malisha's body wrapped up in a blanket that was burnt like charcoal. Kate took the bundle and started squawlin. She fell down on the ground.

Bo and Stump carried her into Daddy's house. Nobody slept for the rest of the night. I buried Malisha's body that afternoon. Everybody watched but nobody said a word.

Ray Fairchild: I can honestly say that I didn't mean to kill anybody, especially a child. A trailer is easy to get out of, and I didn't think it would burn so fast. I... I... I...

Pete Boise: And we have all agreed that the past is the past. I didn't mean to kill Donnie, but that's what happened.

Ray Fairchild: Yeah, that's what happened. After I set Kate and Maurice's trailer on fire, I went back through the woods to my car and back to the hospital. Brother and Sister Edwards spent the night with us in the waiting room. They knew there was something we were not telling them, but they didn't ask. Sister Edwards, who is a pretty lady with blonde hair and big teeth, put her arms around each one of us and cried. Brother Edwards kept calm but tears came to his eyes several times.

Donnie died late in the afternoon. Right after he died, Daddy told Brother and Sister Edwards that he wanted to be alone with the family, and they left us. When they were gone, Daddy said we were going by the hardware store on the way home to stock up on ammunition. We were going to war.

Pete Boise: At the same time Junior was sayin' that to his family, Daddy told us to load all our guns. As soon as the Fairchilds came home, for Malisha's sake, we would kill'em all. We were going to war.

Ray Fairchild: We didn't go directly to the house. We decided to surround them without them knowin' it. We parked our vehicles on the south side of the property and went into the woods. It was getting dark so we wouldn't be seen.

Pete Boise: At the same time, we put on our huntin's camo and spread out in the woods. We wanted to be ready when they got there. We were all in the woods.

Ray Fairchild: Then it sounded like a truck came down the dirt road. Its lights were on and in the dusk you couldn't make out its shape, but we were sure it was some of the Boises.

Pete Boise: We were sure it was the Fairchilds. It stopped in the middle of the road between our houses, and when the driver got out, we opened fire.

Ray Fairdchild: And so did we. His body fell. Then we heard a woman's voice crying from the vehicle, "Please don't shoot! Please." It was Sister Edwards.

Pete Boise: I threw my gun down and turned on my flashlight. It was the church van. I walked toward Brother Edwards.

Ray Fairchild: I did the same and so did everyone else. Brother Edwards was layin' on the ground and he wasn't movin'. Sister Edwards was running her hands over his face and chest and cryin, "He's dead."

"Maybe not," Bose Boise said. "Get back in the van." We all picked him up and laid him on the front bench-style passenger seat. Daddy cranked it up, and we all got in. Back to Springhill Hospital we went.

Pete Boise: Nobody said anything as we went.

Ray Fairchild: My friend Angel Bonsecour was back on duty. She was working the night shift. She checked him for a heartbeat, and he had one. They put him on life support, and Angel came and told us not to worry, that she'd seen a lot worse. She said she saw a guy one time who was completely dead and came back, and Brother Edwards was breathing fine and his heart was beating. She asked if we knew who did it and why anybody would want to shoot Brother Edwards. We all just looked at each other and didn't say anything.

Pete Boise: The Law came about thirty minutes later and started asking questions. The doctor dug five bullets from Brother Edwards' body— a thirty-aught-six, a nine millimeter, a three-o-eight, a twenty-two, and a thirty-thirty— five different kinds. We knew not to answer questions. That's how you get yourself in trouble. No matter what they asked, we said we didn't know.

Ray Fairchild: Sister Edwards said she didn't know either, and she was tellin' the truth. She didn't know what we had done.

Pete Boise: But she had suspicions, and her suspicions were right. She told us what her suspicions were after the police left, and we all confessed that she was right. We had gone to war and Brother Edwards had been caught in the crossfire.

Ray Fairchild: She said she knew things were going bad down the dirt road because our kids had said things that made her and Brother Edwards worry for us all. When Donnie died, they went home but decided they needed to come talk to us about making up and were going to start with the Boises. They would help us all work it out when we came home.

Pete Boise: And I guess they did help us work it out. When Brother Edwards came to, the police came back, but Brother Edwards said he didn't know what happened and wouldn't press charges even if he did.

Ray Fairchild: Then we all felt ashamed— ashamed for what we had done but mostly ashamed that we were not like Brother Edwards. But he told us not to feel ashamed, that there was no purpose in bearing shame. He said how he'd been worse than any of us in his younger days, said how he used to go to bars just to fight and how he was a different man now.

Pete Boise: And for the first time in my life I understood Brother and Sister Edwards and all their talk about souls.

Ray Fairchild: We did a great deal of crying after that. When Brother Edwards got out of the hospital he performed a proper funeral both for the baby and Donnie— both at the same time. Brother Edwards was preaching at his church again in a few weeks, and all of us— Fairchilds and Boises—got baptized and started going to services.

Pete Boise: And we gave up growin' weed and got real jobs.

Ray Fairchild: And we opened up the end of the dirt road for anybody that wanted to come see us.

THE KEY TO THE CITY

ONE

It's not worth the money, this job. When I got it, I thought it would be a stepping stone to something bigger, but after all this time, I'm pretty sure I'm not going anywhere. As the fourth term mayor of a small town, what drives me insane, absolutely hair-pulling insane is the little things. If there's one thing you don't want in a small town, it's strife. Little fires turn into big fires in a hurry so you spend half your time as mayor putting out little fires.

For instance, during my second term, old man Baxter's widow, Hazel Anne, came to me privately to complain about a dog that was barking at her window every night at exactly 2:12 a.m. I told her to speak to Todd Thorson, our part-time animal control officer, and she said she had already and he had told her that if it was a stray, he'd catch him sooner or later and if not, well, he didn't work at two in the morning.

I stayed up late that night. At 1:45 A.M., I parked my truck just down the street from Mrs. Baxter's window. I nearly fell asleep, but at 2:15 (by my watch), the yapping started. It began as a high-pitched, rapid-fire bark, then trailed into a long, slow whine—the kind of bark that makes you want to scream, "Shut up!"

I turned on my headlights and recognized Charlemagne, the furry white and tan, half poodle, half basset hound (I kid you not) that belonged to Dr. James McGurnsey. Why did it have to be his dog? Dr. McGurnsey, with his gray whiskers and rectangular spectacles, makes me nervous. He keeps to himself. He's been here forever. No one knows much about him except maybe his maid. She says he has so many books in his house that there's barely room to walk. He never smiles or frowns, and he speaks in a low voice that is both authoritative and mumbling. When I started first grade, he gave me my shots, and to this day, I hate to admit, I can't so much as look at him without my guts churning.

I whistled and Charlemagne, expecting a treat, I'm sure, came running to me. I lifted him into the bed of my truck and drove to Doc McGurnsey's. I leaned over the chain-link fence and placed Charlemagne on the grass as gently as if he had been a porcelain statue. As I walked back to my truck, I thought about diplomatic ways to inform Doc of the situation, but before I had taken five steps, I heard the chain-link fence rattling, turned, and saw Charlemagne climbing it like it was monkey bars and he was a monkey.

Just then Doc's porch light came on.

"Uh, who's there?" I heard Doc ask in a gruff, sleepy voice.

"It's Monty Jordan," I said.

"Uh, Monty? What are you doing out there at, uh, this time of the morning?"

A diplomatic, but entirely unbelievable answer popped into my head. "Well, you see, it's Charlemagne I'm worried about. He's climbing your fence."

"I'll take care of it," Doc said. His porch light went out. His door closed. Two days later a white picket fence, the new kind, made of vinyl, stood in place of the chain link and Charlemagne's nocturnal wandering was a problem solved.

Did anyone thank me? Of course not. How am I doing as mayor? I never really know.

I was keeping folks happy, I thought, but a few months

back, maybe a year, something went wrong in Clegmore—horribly wrong. The town started falling apart. Everyone was pointing fingers at everyone else (especially at me), but no one could say exactly what was happening.

TWO

I remember when the first thing went wrong. I remember it because I remember what I was doing. Every village has at least one idiot. Clegmore has had several, and the worst was Mrs. Luvy Mitchell's half-retarded son, Roy. Luvy and Roy lived in Bozell's Trailer Park in the northwest quadrant of town, and when Luvy died that left Roy to tend to himself, which he wasn't able to do. He ended up wandering in the streets, wearing orange, red, and blue suits, a cowboy hat and tennis shoes, and carrying a stick with a nail on the end for spearing aluminum cans. He would get right up in folks' faces and start talking about stuff that no one understood, and something had to be done. Doc McGurnsey examined him and had him temporarily assigned to a nursing facility on the other end of the county. Folks said he needed to be sent off to a mental institution. I had no authority in the matter, but I was indirectly connected to three of the four county and state agencies that did, and some of the paperwork was sent to my desk.

I was going through his documents when it happened. I glanced out my office window, which faces Main Street, and saw two men shouting at each other and about to come to blows. I recognized both men. They had owned shops next to each other for at least ten years.

There was no time to think. I dashed down the stairs, ran out the door and got between them just as they were squaring off.

"Whoa. Wait a minute, Richard, Harvey. Get hold of yourselves. What's going on here?" I asked.

"It's that sign," Richard Leighton screamed, pointing at the coffee and doughnuts sign hanging over the door to Harvey Dew's storefront. "It blocks the street-view of my business! Unless you're walking down the sidewalk, you can't see my shop!"

"That sign's been there five years, and you haven't said a word," Harvey yelled back. "If your business has got problems, it's because of that gang of thugs you call repairmen that run it, and having them around is hurting every business on this street. Who needs an appliance repair shop anymore anyway? Why don't you give up and sell this eyesore?"

"Gentlemen, gentlemen," I said, "please, let's talk this thing out. Come up to my office."

They stepped back from each other and followed me inside and up the stairs. They sat in the leather chairs that faced my desk, and for a minute, neither said anything. They relaxed and their breathing became even.

"I'm sorry," Richard said. "I don't know what came over me. Your sign doesn't block the view to my shop at all, and the better you do, the more customers I have. I'm sorry."

"Yeah, me too," Harvey replied. "I don't know why I said that about your guys. They're good customers of mine. They come in for coffee every morning. I really don't know what came over me out there."

They spoke for a few more seconds, and I asked, "So everything's okay now?"

"Yeah," they both said.

They left, and I thought another little problem had been solved and that all would be well in Clegmore, Alabama, but I could not have been more wrong. The next day as I was having lunch at Grandma's Kitchen, a country restaurant on the north side of town, I heard glass crashing on the floor in the smoking section.

"I am not picking that up!" Faith Petree screamed, "And I am not waiting on you ever again, you dirty old man."

"Well, who needs you?" Tate Wilson grunted. "You're the slowest waitress in town."

I knew Faith to be one of the best waitresses ever and Tate to be a gentleman, in a countrified way, so I could not believe what I was hearing.

Faith's manager, Mrs. Avera Delchamp, came out from the back and demanded, "What's going on out here?"

Faith and Tate tried to explain at the same time, but before either finished, Avera said, "Okay, here's what we'll do. This is going to be simple enough. Tate, you get out of here right now, never mind your bill, and never come into this restaurant again. Faith, you are fired."

I couldn't believe it. Faith had been at Grandma's Kitchen for as long as there had been a Grandma's Kitchen. When I got back to my desk, Don Fosky, proprietor of my old business, an office supply shop, called. I had sold him the business two years ago and the transition to his ownership had been as smooth as kitten's fur. But he was telling me that if I didn't do something about the floor he was suing me.

"The floor? What's wrong with the floor?"

"It's hardwood. It's warped. There's knots in it."

"I'll be right over," I said.

When I got there, Don had calmed down. "I'm sorry, Monty. I don't know what came over me. The floor's fine. It's eighty years old, an antique. For goodness sake, you didn't have to come over."

"That's alright," I said, and for a few minutes we both

stood in awkward silence.

Then I asked, "Are you feeling okay?"

"I don't know," Don said. "Maybe it's the weather."

I thought his answer over. Yes, that had to be it. It seemed like it had been overcast a lot lately. I thought things would get better when the weather improved... but that's not the way it happened.

THREE

Bozell's Trailer Park is a scattered collection of rusty cracker cans. "Trashy" is the word most people, including those who live there, use to describe it.

Half the calls to our police department are from Bozell's. A couple of weeks after the first angry incidents, I was sure that things had calmed down, but Tommy Black, Clegmore's police chief, came to me to request funding for hiring additional officers because, as he put it, "Bozell's has turned into 'bo-hell'. There's three times as many fights and break-ins, and now there's destruction of property."

"Destruction of property?"

"Yeah, Matt Duffy got his Trans Am burned. Somebody poured gasoline on it. His mother had a brick thrown through her kitchen window. Three dogs have been shot. One trailer got pushed off its blocks.

All my officers are pulling overtime, and a couple are about to snap."

"I'll have to go to the council," I said, "and we don't have another meeting until next week."

For a moment his face turned blood red, and he started to say something, but he drew a deep breath and released it slowly.

"Yes sir," he whispered, and it sounded like he was

choking on the words.

He left, and I found myself feeling... what's the word? You know how you feel when you're watching a stock car race and the front car starts to spin and you know there's going to be a pile-up? That's how I felt.

FOUR

But there was no pile-up. There wasn't even a crash. Instead, things went in the opposite direction, which is not to say that they improved— far from it.

What came out in violent eruptions at first seemed to become internalized and a heavy gloom set in. I first noticed it in Fran, my wife. Fran and I have never had a problem with communication. In thirty years of marriage, we've had lots of little arguments and even a couple of big fights, but we've always kept the line open.

A month or so after the eruptions, I went home from work one afternoon, asked Fran about her day, and she didn't answer.

"Fran," I raised my voice, "how was your day?"

She stared into space.

I moved my hand in front of her face. She slowly turned to look at me, but her eyes seemed fixed on something behind my head.

"Just nothing," she said under her breath.

"What?"

In an even quieter voice she said, "nothing" and turned her face away.

I moved around her so that we stood face to face and tried to speak, but she was in no mood. Later that night we spoke for a few minutes, but the next night she was in the same silent mood.

I thought she was just tired, but after a few weeks of her going in and out of this mood, I knew something had changed.

I suppose I would have rushed my wife to a psychiatrist, but she wasn't the only one that had changed.

Lisa Gulliver, a cashier at Farmer's Consolidated Bank, didn't answer me one afternoon until I had called her name three times. Everyone started drifting and disconnecting themselves from each other. Several times I found myself driving along in my truck, not sure where I was going or how long I had been driving.

I went to the dentist, and after he placed a bib around my neck and opened my mouth, he sat with two of his fingers hanging on my bottom lip for thirty minutes as he stared out the window.

I didn't know what to do for the town. Maybe we could have more sporting events or try to get new industry in. We were bored, I thought, and if we remedied that, things would be okay, but as I was pondering the problem, the town changed again.

FIVE

Three things started happening at once. Long time residents began to move away. Strangers began to move in, and Clegmore's appearance changed.

With the exception of Bozell's Trailer Park, Clegmore was the kind of town that might have inspired a Norman Rockwell painting. The brick buildings on Main Street were seventy to one hundred years old, but well-kept. The barber shops, the manicured lawns, the cracked but well swept sidewalks, the post office, the schools, the library and the churches—all spoke of order and care. It was the kind of place where people put down roots, but something in the balance of who was moving in and who was moving out got tilted.

Folks who had been born here and had lived here their whole lives put their houses up for sale. I asked several where they were planning to move to, but none had definite plans. They just wanted out of Clegmore.

Perhaps their moving away would not have been so bad, but the folks who were buying their houses weren't just strangers, they were strange. I don't mean "strange-cool," I mean "strange-bad." It's not that they were all of the same sort—some were drug heads, but most were not. Some drove loud vehicles and played their stereos loud, but most did not. Some left junk scattered on their lawns, but most did not. The only common thread was a sickening creepiness that I can't explain. For instance, one of them had a stray dog take up residence under his house, but instead of going to Todd Thorson, he shot the dog with a rifle.

Their presence tipped a balance in the town, and others stopped caring. Lawns that had once been pictures of perfection with rows of bright pink flowers and one-inch tall grass were now covered with trash. Weeds grew tall. Broken glass was scattered on the streets and sidewalks.

The only good thing left about our town was the strength of its economy, but that changed too.

SIX

Economies of towns like ours are built on retirement checks and a small handful of industries. We had three industries. The biggest and most important was a factory that made elastic for underwear. If you would like to know where the underwear you've got on this very minute got its springiness, well, there's a good chance it got it from us. When other garment factories were closing, ours remained open because it was also a shipping hub for the corporation. We're close to an interstate highway, you see, and for that reason, our second industry was trucking. We had a few independent truckers, but more importantly we had a growing trucking company on the north side of town. The third industry was a small manufacturer of replacement transmission parts.

The garment factory left first. Despite repeated promises never to do so, it moved its offices to Atlanta and production facilities to Honduras. The transmission parts producer left second. Steel prices, their president said, were better in South America and labor was cheaper. Besides, he said, Clegmore didn't seem to want the company around.

The trucking company didn't leave, but it lost two of its largest contracts in one week, and the company half died. That left the retirement checks, and the only local business that seemed to thrive was the hospital.

Folks were looking to blame someone, and naturally, many were ready to have my head on a platter. That is when I decided to call a town meeting.

When the date of the meeting rolled around, it rained all day. I sipped liquid antacid, and my mouth tasted like chalk.

SEVEN

Minutes of the Clegmore Town Meeting

February 21, 200_. Mayor Monty Jordan presiding. Gayle Quarrell, recording secretary. Transfer from Audiotape.

Mayor Monty Jordan: I called this meeting to discuss the

decline in our town. This is an open-forum discussion, but I ask each of you to speak in turn only as you are recognized. Please use the microphones at the end of the aisles. I see some of you lining up, and I can tell you're... well... eager. Just be kind. That's all I ask. The chair recognizes Floyd Amerson at microphone number eight.

Floyd Amerson: Monty, you and I have known each other since we were boys. We played football together at Clegmore High. I don't want you to take what I'm about to say personally, but, well, everybody knows the problem, plain and simple. It's you! You never were right for this job, and it's time you resign.

(Applause and voiced agreement in audience)

Yeah, that's right. You were in over your head from day one (applause), and you need to let somebody else take the job. (applause)

Not that you're a bad fellow or anything, nothing personal.

Mayor Monty Jordan: Thank you, Floyd. I would like to address your suggestion, if I may. As you know, I'm in my fourth term as mayor—been doing this job for nearly fifteen years now. For all of this time, I have carried out my duties pretty much the same way. In the last two elections, I've run unopposed, and for thirteen years there have been few complaints. It's only in the last year that things have changed. If I had changed my way of doing things, I would be to blame, and I would resign, but I haven't changed. (muffled applause, small amount of voiced agreement in audience)
Wait, though. I honestly don't think I am to blame, but if

it is the opinion of the majority attending this meeting that I am the problem, I will resign upon the conclusion of this meeting and pass the gavel to Linda Delchamp, vice chairperson of the town council. First, let's give everybody a chance to talk. The chair recognizes Myra Smith.

Myra Smith: Since I'm the director of the public library and as such, a city employee, perhaps it is a conflict of interest that I speak, but I would like to address the gathering if no one disagrees.

Mayor Monty Jordan: There appears to be no disagreement. You may address the meeting.

Myra Smith: First off, I would like to say that I think you're doing a fine job, Mayor Jordan, but you brought up one point about what you do and what everyone in this town does that, I think, is the problem. This town resists change. When I came here two years ago, right out of college, the library still had not installed a computerized materials checkout system. Clegmore never changes. It's turned in on itself and is not progressive. It's that simple. We must embrace change.

Mayor Monty Jordan: Thank you, Myra. Would anyone care to speak to Mrs. Smith's concern? Yes? The chair recognizes Doris Hobbes at microphone number three.

Doris Hobbes: I'm ninety-four years old. Been living in this town since I turned eighteen and married Theodore Hobbes, my departed husband. I don't know exactly how long that's been, and I'm too old to add it up in my head, but it's been awhile.

I knew somebody would blame this town's problems on

us not changing. They always do, but I tell you this town's changed plenty! Granted, we ain't New York City, and we don't let ourselves get pushed around by every new breeze that blows through, but change we have!

I can remember when the streets were dirt and people drove mule carts into town. I can remember houses without running water and the outhouses behind them. I can remember when we got electricity, then gas, then garbage pickup. I remember the first red light and the first electric railroad crossing gate. I watched a John Wayne movie the first night the theater opened and watched the same movie on television when the first cable TV wires were laid. When they built the airstrip on the east side of town, my husband sold the city eighty acres from his daddy's old farm.

Clegmore is careful and doesn't change every time the wind shifts directions, but change it does.

I say all this just to say that we don't want to rush off in some senseless new direction just for the sake of doing it. We might need to change, but let's be careful!
(Loud applause erupts in audience. Some stand and cheer.)

Mayor Monty Jordan: Thank you, Doris. The chair recognizes Richard Leighton at microphone number four.

Richard Leighton: I submit that we need a better infrastructure for industry. Industry is what drives the economy, and a good economy is the key to everything else being good. We are suffering an economic breakdown. That's all. Why don't we appoint a committee to study and improve our economic infrastructure?
Mayor Monty Jordan: Would anyone care to address Richard's concern? (No answer) Thank you, Richard, your concern is noted and may be brought up in the second portion of the meeting. The chair recognizes Hal Bozell.

Hal Bozell: To some of you idealistic college types, what I'm about to say is going to sound prejudiced, but I don't care. I've been running a trailer park in this town for twenty-seven years, and I've become acquainted with the lowest forms of human trash. I don't live in the park, myself. In fact, there's not enough money in the world to pay me to live there. I don't mind talking like this about my tenants because, as you might expect, not even one of them has cared enough to attend this meeting. So no harm done.

Here's the thing: Trash is trash. People don't change. All this town needs is stronger zoning laws and stronger law enforcement. If people insist on being trash, you gotta treat'em that way. What this town needs is to be tough.

(A few loud claps in the audience followed by a complete hush and several seconds of silence as Dr. James McGurnsey stands. Hal Bozell and others at microphones sit down.)

Mayor Monty Jordan: The chair recognizes Dr. James McGurnsey.

Dr. James McGurnsey: My training and, uh, lifelong career has been in science, hard science if you will, and, uh, as a student of science, I have rejected most, if not all, uh, metaphysical explanations of events.

But that being said, I have seen a few things over the years, darned few, that...well... they were, uh, strange, for lack of a better word. Uh, like the time a young woman who lived out by the railroad tracks, who waited tables in the daytime and sold popcorn and, uh, cleaned up at the movie theater at night, crashed a Buick into a dairy truck, head on, and fell into, uh, a coma. That was in 1973. Not much was known about comas in those days. We tried to wake her up—tried everything. We made noise. We massaged her. We poured ice water on her. We even tried, uh, shocking her. Nothing happened.

She didn't have a husband, but she had a four-year-old son. Her mother kept him at their family farm because she didn't want him to see her in that condition. When her condition started going downhill fast and we were sure she didn't have long, her mother thought we should bring the boy in just so he could, uh, see her one last time. Nobody at the hospital, myself included, thought it would be a good idea—could have scarred the boy, you know—but the woman insisted and we had, uh, no choice but to let her bring him.

I was standing by the bed when she brought him. She picked him up and lowered him onto his mother's, uh, bosom. When the boy touched his mothers face, for the first time in two months, mind you, he burst out crying and said, "Mama, I have missed you. I didn't think you were ever coming back. Don't ever leave me again, Mama."

I didn't see her eyes open, but before the last word left his mouth, she was looking right at him. In a dry voice that sounded more like, uh, a frog croaking than a human being talking, she said, "Mama's here, baby, and Mama's never going to leave you again."

And so, her coma ended. Coincidence? Miracle? Something in between? Who am I to say? These things, whatever they are, don't happen often, mind you. But what am I talking about? I began to notice things after that, began to explore a science that is not a science. Are there causes and effects that are not related? Why is it that a man can study music at the best schools in the world, practice for thirty years, get a symphony recorded and no one buys it, but a backwoods drifter with nothing but a dime-store guitar and a half empty whiskey bottle can cut

a record that sells a million copies? How is it that everyone who's had geometry knows what a circle is and knows
what a diameter is but no one has ever defined the relationship of a circle to its diameter, not even with all the
computers in the world combined? It's an irrational number, and that's what I'm talking about. Irrational knowl-
edge and well...

I said all that to say this. I think the problem is, no, I
feel the problem is, that's the best word "feel," but that's
not quite right either, uh... I believe the problem with
Clegmore is this: About a year ago a mildly retarded man
named Roy Mitchell was sent away. I'm not sure how or
why that is the problem, but that's it. That's the problem.

(Dr. James McGurnsey sits. The audience is silent. Five
minutes pass.)

Mayor Monty Jordan: If no one else wishes to address the
meeting, we will adjourn. Your concerns will be presented at
the next town council meeting. Anyone else? Anyone? No.

(Mayor Jordan strikes podium with gavel.)

The meeting is adjourned.

EIGHT

That was a little more than two months ago. After the
meeting, several of the town council members asked me if
we needed to call the council together for a special session,
but I said we didn't. I told them we would get Roy back,
and I didn't think there was anything to discuss. The

council members agreed, and I started the process the same night by calling a friend of mine who is a state judge.

The process has been slow. We located a relative of Roy's in Texas and only by much pleading did we convince her to authorize his papers. Before she signed, two council members had to drive all the way out there, treat her to lunch and supper, and promise that she or her children would receive all of Roy's possessions when he passed.

Roy won't be here for at least another month, but the town is already improving—recovering faster than it got sick. Of course it could just be a coincidence. Maybe the downward cycle had reached its conclusion, and the town would have begun to come around anyway.

But if bringing Roy back is the thing that's rejuvenating our town, well, I suppose stranger things have happened. I've pondered for an explanation. Maybe having somebody to look down on keeps people feeling good about themselves—or maybe it humbles them. Maybe having one person for everyone to despise keeps people from despising each other. Or maybe, as Doc put it, it's metaphysical. Maybe there are so many angels assigned to protect fools that having a fool around shields the rest of us from evil.

Well, I wouldn't bet on any of it, but I tell you what I am going to do as soon as Roy Boy (that's his nickname) comes home. He's fond of wearing gaudy ornaments around his neck like Mardi Gras beads or fake gold chains. I'm going to give him a trinket to hang on a real gold chain. I'm giving him the key to the city.

The author invites you to visit his website:
www.shepherdsheart.info
You may contact the author directly at
Rhett@shepherdsheart.info

Do not miss:

The Wisdom of Shepherds

the masterpiece by Rhett Ellis

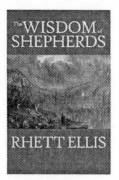

The *Wisdom of Shepherds* is the story of Old Caleb the shepherd. One winter he returns to the crumbling cottage he has used for shelter for fifty years and hears a strange voice singing a strange song. He fears that the mysterious singer has unearthed the secret thing he buried beneath the cottage when he was a young man. He knocks on the cottage door, and a woman with red hair opens it.

What follows is a humorous, good-natured yarn full of powerful emotion, wisdom, and fun.

Printed in the United States
36009LVS00002B/7-12